The Love We Had

A NOVELLA

A NOVEL BY *Myriah*

Hey a!
Thanks for the support! I hope you
enjoy!

-Myriah

© 2019

Published by Miss Candice Presents

All rights reserved.

This is a work of fiction.

Names, characters, businesses, places, events and incidents
are either the products of the author's imagination or used in a
fictitious manner.

Any resemblance to actual persons, living or dead, or actual
events is purely coincidental.

Unauthorized reproduction, in any manner, is prohibited

Acknowledgements

Whew! First and foremost, I'd like to thank God for giving me the patience. I had a plan to drop a book a month and as you guys can see, that did not pan out the way that I had hoped. But my real readers stuck with me and for that, I am about to come through! Thank you for rocking with me and I hope you enjoy The Love We Had as much as I enjoyed writing it. This book caused me tears, frustration and after 5,000 re-writes, I am finally satisfied with the work I've produced so I hope that you are as well. Peyton and Princeton's love story is one for the birds. The doves and the lovebirds.

My special shout-out goes to everyone who has stuck with me through the discouragement and all of the slacking that I've been doing. I hope that you all are down for the ride that is about to come when it comes to my work. If this is the first book that you're reading from me, I hope that it will nourish and quench the thirst you have for a pure, romance novel. By name I have to thank, my publisher first. I couldn't have done any of this without you. They better watch out. #MCP is nothing to play with.

To the person who has given me the most motivation throughout this whole thing; Natasha Lathan. My chocolate! I'm so blessed to have you in my life and thank God for you everyday. You don't get mad at me for not writing and you are the only person who knows my feelings through and through. For every tear, you've been there. Every vent and every rant, you've never turned your back on me. I appreciate you more than you could ever understand. This book is for you.

To my angel, life without you is hard but I know one day, things will start looking up. I hope that "one day" comes very soon. To my mommy, I can't wait to catch up with you. I hope you're proud up there since I didn't get a chance to do it while you were down here with me.

With love and peace,
Myriah.

Chapter One

"NO ONE KNOWS THE PAIN."
PEYTON TAHJ EVER.

Peyton Tahj Ever; that's what my parents named me, and for eighteen long years, that's who I was. But, not anymore. As of two weeks ago, on November 20th 2017 at 7:04 A.M, I am Taylen Ella Tahj Ever's mommy. A lot of shit had happened, but none of that even mattered any more. All that mattered now was getting my daughter and I away from the home where I thought I was safe. After hearing my boyfriend's mom talking on the phone in the middle of the night, I knew that there was no way that I could continue living there, knowing that she was about to try and take my daughter from me.

Shushing Taylen as I changed her diaper so that she wouldn't fuss, I put her in a thick onesie and swaddled her in two blankets. It was cold as fuck in Rhode Island and that's one of the reasons I knew I needed to get the fuck out of here. I never liked it here but for some reason, I let Talon, my daughter's father, talk me into moving here to be close to his family, isolating my own in the process. There was no way that my parents would allow me to come back, especially not after all the fucked up shit I had said, so that was not an option. Laying Tay on the bed and placing pillows around her so that she wouldn't fall, I creeped into Talon's mom's room and praised God when I saw the opened, almost-empty bottle of sleeping pills on her nightstand. Her purse was always at the foot of the bed so tip-toeing as close to Ms. Shondell as I could get without getting scared, I snatched it off and then hid in the bathroom, quietly rummaging through it until I found her wallet. Her bourgeois ass always carried cash, so I pocketed the $400, and then returned her purse. Once I snatched her phone off the charger, I quickly left the room.

Jumping, I could have sworn that I heard noise coming from the kitchen so I peeked to make sure that it wasn't Shondell's baldheaded, nosey daughter Shondae. Then, I quickly relaxed when I heard her snoring coming from the bedroom next to mine. Strapping the baby carrier onto my chest, I quickly put Taylen inside of it, knowing that my luck was probably about to run out. I was starting to get sore, still recovering from having my daughter naturally and ripping. Making sure that she was comfortable and warm, I put a coat over us. It was easily 30 degrees outside and I was not going to risk her getting sick. When I was certain that we were ready, I hoisted the bag over my shoulder and then creeped down the stairs, wincing every time that they creaked. Reaching the bottom step, I noticed that someone had put one of my favorite pictures of Talon on the mural they had in their home, so I snatched it off and put it in my bag. Quietly unlocking the front door, I knew that the alarm would sound, but since nobody had ever felt uncomfortable enough to give it to me, that was just a risk I was going to have to take. The moment I opened the door, I bolted and though I thought I could make it, I realized I wasn't moving nearly as fast as I thought I was, so I quickly ducked behind one of the houses. I had held my daughter close to me so that she wouldn't be bounced so much and when I checked on her to make sure she was okay, her mouth was agape. Despite the circumstances, I couldn't help but chuckle because she looked so much like her dad, as if I hadn't done all the work. That's when the tears came and with my hormones still raging, it was hard to keep them under control. When Tay started to fuss though, I quickly put my big girl panties back on and walked out of the neighborhood. Luckily, a taxi was driving right past me and probably astonished that I was traveling with a baby in this weather, he quickly pulled over.

"Umm... ma'am, I can't take you guys without a carseat for your baby." I could tell that the man was serious but there was no way that I was going to risk going back to that house and Shondell snatching my baby right from my arms, so I started my theatrics in hopes that it would work. All I had to do was start crying and blubbering incoherently. But when he saw me start to "hyperventilate", he really lost it. "It's okay. It's okay. Just put your seatbelt on. Where do you need to go?" he asked. That's when I calmed down, and wiped the tears from my face dramatically.

"The nearest bus station, please. I need to get out of Rhode Island."

Since it was clear that going back to Boston was out of the question, I knew that I only had one other option. I needed to make my way to Cleveland where my older brother Dante lived. My parents had disowned me for sure, but Dante would never do that to me. So paying for my ticket quickly, I got on the bus and prepared for the 30-hour drive, with a newborn. Luckily, Taylen was still sleep so I shut my eyes too, knowing that it wouldn't last long.

I was right. Not even an hour later, Taylen was crying hysterically, and nothing I was doing was working. Laying her in the seat next to me since the bus wasn't packed, I put a blanket down and quickly changed her diaper. The road was bumpy so I held my baby's chest so that she couldn't fall. When she was all changed and dry again, I tried to rock her but that didn't even work. That was the first moment where I really doubted my choice to leave the safety of Shondell's home. Maybe she could take care of my baby better than me. Once that thought presented itself, I realized that I really was losing my mind. Nobody in the world could take care of my baby better than me. After almost 41 weeks of pregnancy and fifty-four hours of labor, there was no way that I was going to do all the work for someone else to raise my child. Especially not Shondell Mason, who had done a horrible job of raising her own children. Talon, my boyfriend, was born at a really rough time in her life and he pretty much raised himself. Shondae was off the wall and when I thought about Taylen ending up that way, I cringed and just continued to walk her.

By this time, Taylen's melt-down, and my upcoming meltdown, were being witnessed by everyone on the bus. Nobody offered me a sympathetic smile or a helping hand even though they saw me struggling. Instead, they preferred to cast judgement on her and cut their eyes at me, as if that was helping me. I already felt shitty enough. But then, I heard the man in the aisle across from me speaking out loud.

"So y'all gonna just stare at her like you never heard a baby cry, huh?" he said loudly. Then, everyone stopped looking and continued to mind their own business. When he noticed that I was struggling trying to balance

Taylen and make a bottle at the same time, he immediately walked over and offered a helping hand. Gratefully, I handed Taylen over and was surprised when he bounced her effortlessly. After only a few moments, she quieted down and I was able to focus on making her bottle. Once I had poured the formula in though, I cursed, realizing that I only had cold water and no way to warm it up. Hoping that the man could offer a solution, I managed to only say a few words. "I can't give my baby a cold bottle."

Handing Taylen back off to me delicately, he walked back to his seat and grabbed his backpack, pulling a thermostat out of it. Whatever reason God had sent this man to me, I was grateful because he grabbed the bottle and poured the water in. It was still steaming hot, so he grabbed my water and poured that in, shaking it up. Like a professional, he tested the milk out on his wrist and then gave it to me. I didn't quite trust him though, and tested it out for myself. I even went so far as to smell it to make sure it smelled like pure formula before I gave it to her.

"Why do you just carry around bottles of hot water?" I asked, nearly melting when he smiled, watching my daughter's eyes close as she ate.

"Drinking tea. But I don't like it when it sits too long, so I always wash my thermal out and add fresh water." He explained. The fact that he drank tea surprised the fuck out of me, but I didn't question it. "Can I hold her?" he asked. Figuring since he'd held her before with no problems, I handed her back to him with no problem. Think what you want to about me. Even moms need a break sometimes.

"Do you have kids?" I asked, already knowing the answer. I was pleasantly surprised when he shook his head.

"No. I guess I've been too busy chasing other things... I never really thought about settling down and starting a family." He confessed. I knew there was more to the story by the way he was staring at my baby. I had a feeling he was lying, but I let it go. That's when he looked up at me, and when our eyes met, he shook his head. "Damn, I'm rude. I'm Princeton Parrish, but everyone calls me P.J." he introduced himself and I analyzed him. Nobody compared to Talon, and I'm sure they never would, but this man was a close second. He looked to be in his late 20's and donned a fitting business suit. I could tell he was some sort of businessman because he had a briefcase under his seat. I thought about giving him a fake name but changed my mind. He was too fine for that.

"I'm Peyton... Peyton Ever. That's my baby girl, Taylen." I smiled politely, trying to hide my nervousness.

"Why are you heading to Cleveland? Visiting family?" he asked, and I immediately shut down. There was no way I was going to put myself in a weird situation, so I thought it was best if he didn't know enough to call CPS on me.

"Yeah. Something like that. What about you?" I asked, looking for a quick escape to the conversation.

"Business, well kind of. My father lives in Cleveland and I'm going down a little early to celebrate with him, but I have a few business meetings to attend while I'm there." He explained and I nodded my head, secretly patting myself on the back. Glancing at the clock, I shook my head as I realized we still had 28 hours of traveling left.

It seemed like a long time, but with Princeton keeping me company, I was hardly looking at the clock. As a matter of fact, my eyes stayed on his lips most of the entire time that he talked, worshipping the way that he used his tongue to swipe the bottom one every so often. We played 21 questions, but with more than a day of traveling to do, 21 turned into 21,000, easily. I learned that he had an older brother, Kingston Jr. and two younger sisters, Angelina and Kyrah. He graduated top 10 of his class at California State and owned a million-dollar entertainment company, alongside his father. His older brother was the PR rep for their company. Angelina was a fashion consultant and Kyrah hadn't graduated college yet, but there was no doubt in Princeton's mind that she would probably fall right in line with the family norm. I also learned that he had no children, which surprised me because of how good he was with my baby.

With seventeen hours hours left of the trip, the bus pulled over to a rest stop and Princeton stood up to stretch, handing me Taylen as he checked his phone. "You hungry? You or the baby need anything?" He asked me. I wanted to play it off, but my stomach was growling for some real food. I'd brought a few snacks along with me, but with no real protein, I was starting to get a hunger headache. I had money with me but I was trying to preserve it for as long as I could, knowing that if I couldn't find Dante, my baby and I would need a place to stay. Before I could answer, my stomach's loud growl gave me away. "Say no more. I got you."

Seeing that a lot of people were getting off the bus, I knew the lines would be long so I gave Taylen a bottle and rocked us both back to sleep. In my head, the quicker we went to sleep, the quicker I could forget about the fact that I was slowly starving to death.

Chapter Two

"BURNING ALL MY BRIDGES."

PRINCETON JAMES PARRISH.

Walking into the corner store, I grabbed bottles of soda, juice, bags of chips and when I approached the counter, I ordered chicken strips, and a burrito. Everyone stared at me in disbelief because I barely flinched at the total as I entered my credit card and waited for it to go through. When that was finished, I grabbed my bags and walked back to the Greyhound bus, boarding it just as my phone began to ring. When I saw that it was Jersey, I cursed under my breath but declined the call. I'd have to call her back later. Approaching Peyton's seat, I almost laughed when I saw her and her baby passed out, like they'd been drinking all night. Nudging her gently, I looked away from her so it wouldn't look like I was staring at the spit rolling down her chin. Peyton barely moved, and then settled right back into her spot, cradling Taylen.

"Peyton, wake up. I got food." When that didn't work, I waved the food under her nose and as the smell went up her nose, she stirred awake and quickly grabbed the food out of my hand like a preying mantis. I've never seen a woman inhale food so fast but she did it like it was nothing and then without another word, wiped her mouth. I handed her the bag of drinks and wasn't surprised when she grabbed the watermelon flavored one. She struck me as someone who liked watermelon.

"Thank you."

Between talking to Peyton and sleeping while they slept, the rest of the trip went by without issue... and it seemed like in no time, we were pulling into Cleveland's city limits. I could tell that Peyton was anxious being in uncharted territory, so I did my best to try to make her feel better.

"You need to use my phone to call someone to come get you from the bus station?" I offered. She didn't know it, but I could feel her feet tapping nervously, so I asked a different question. "I can drive you somewhere? Anywhere, actually. Just give me an address." I explained, hitting her with the sly smirk that got everyone. Except it didn't work on Peyton. She blushed until her cheeks became dark and flushed.

"I don't have an address..." she responded, but I knew she wanted to say something else so I remained quiet. "Honestly Princeton, I have no idea what I'm doing. I just know that nothing can happen to my baby, so I'm going to do what I have to do to keep her safe." For the first time, I sensed brutal honesty in her voice. All I could see was a desperate, but prideful mother. There was no way that she was going to ask for my help so I was going to have to just give it to her.

"Well, I definitely understand that... so I'll tell you this. My company is putting me in the Westin. Let me put you and your daughter there too... and by the time I leave, hopefully we will have found your brother." Peyton's face lit up, but then she thought of something and her hopes diminished again. "If we can't find him, we'll figure something else out. I promise." I refused to allow her to sit around and reflect on whatever it was that was bothering her, so I grabbed her by the hand and as we got off the bus, I led her to the black car that my office had waiting for me. Unknown to her, I was hoping that she would agree to my offer long before we even came to Cleveland, so I had the driver stop and pick up a car seat, knowing they would refuse to take Peyton and her baby anywhere if she didn't have one.

When we pulled into the parking lot of the Westin, I immediately got out and grabbed everything so that Peyton wouldn't have to carry anything but Taylen. I realized the time and cursed under my breath. I barely had time to get ready for my next meeting, let alone spend time with Peyton

THE LOVE WE HAD

and Taylen. After getting them set up in their room, I went to mine to take a shower and change.

An hour later, I was in the back of the car and on my way to the business meeting. I hit decline on every single one of KJ's calls, because him calling me wasn't about to make a nigga get there faster. He kept calling but as his name flashed across the screen, I was pulling in so I declined it again.

Sitting in the conference room with a bunch of my comrades, my father, and our clients, I was slightly paying attention, but my mind was on Peyton. I spent my time wondering if she'd eaten, or what her and the baby were doing so the moment that we got a break, I stepped away to call the room. It rang for awhile and right when I was about to hang up, I heard her sweet voice come over the speakers.

"Peyton!" I called, my voice becoming more excited than I anticipated. Trying to play it cool, I cleared my throat and tried it again. "What are you doing? How's the baby?" I asked, smiling when I heard her laugh.

"You just left, Princeton…." She chuckled and by how deep her voice was, I could tell she had been sleeping.

"My bad, I didn't mean to wake you up, mama. I just wanted to tell you to order whatever you want to eat, it's on my tab." I heard her sighing but was afraid of what she'd say if I asked her what was wrong so I stayed quiet. "Peyton?" I questioned, after a long moment of silence.

"I'll just wait for you, Prince. I don't wanna spend your money. I'm not hungry." She responded. Before I could ask her anything else, she hung up and I stared at the phone in disbelief. I wasn't sure what was wrong with her, but if she was hungry and refused to fix the problem, I'd do it for her. Picking the phone back up, I called the Westin's kitchen and ordered everything off the menu that I thought she would like. By the time I finished, it was time to get back to my meeting so I sat down and focused, even though my mind was completely on Peyton. My dad must have been able to tell I was preoccupied because after the meeting finally ended, he came up and put his hand on my shoulder.

"Princeton, what's going on, son? You seem distracted. How was your flight?" Kingston, my dad, asked. My father and I never had a good relationship, mostly because he spent the most of his time traveling with other women while my mother stayed at home and cared for us. But as I got older and realized how much he sacrificed just for my siblings and I to have a pretty decent life, I did my best to stitch together our bond. The last four years hadn't been a breeze especially since Pops was so similar to me and us working together was a struggle, but we made it happen. One of the things that we had in common was our mutual love of money.

"It got delayed... They couldn't get me on another flight until tomorrow and since I knew that I had to be here today to present, I rode on the Greyhound." The disgust on my father's face was apparent but I did my best to ignore him. My father may have forgotten where he came from, but my mom had always taught me to be humble and grateful, for everything.

"The greyhound, huh?" He spat, his face twisted up as if he'd just taken a spoonful of lemon juice. "No wonder you're in a bad mood." My dad mumbled under his breath, probably thinking that I couldn't hear him.

"Actually, it wasn't bad. I met this girl, dad.... On the bus. Her and her baby.... I can't explain it, but she needed some help. I did what you would have done. I put her up in a room and bought her some food." I explained, feeling the uncomfortable silence as my dad went to sit back in his chair. I knew one of his lectures was coming, so I took inhaled a deep breath, just in case he tried to get under my skin.

"Princeton, son... I only want what's best for you. You know that. It's always been like that. You've had the best of everything since the moment you came into this world. Why would you squander all that away to help someone you don't even know?" I couldn't give him an answer, because I was still trying to figure it out myself. So I averted his gaze and looked out the window, watching as everyone appeared as small as ants. If I gave him the real reason, he'd probably think I was crazy, so I kept my mouth shut. Unfortunately, sometimes I thought my dad knew me better than I knew myself, and this was one of those times. "Don't tell me you like this girl, Princeton James." When he said my full name, I instantly thought of my mother and clenched my teeth. He probably knew that made me mad, so he softened his tone and cleared his throat, starting over. "P.J, man.... Don't let this suit fool you. You know the hood that I came from and how many bridges I've burned to get our empire to this statute... To this level. I gave up everything for this life and will not allow anyone to mess this up for our family... Not you, and certainly not some homeless hoe looking for charity, or someone to have a new baby by so she can find a better meal ticket. Maybe she could tell by the suit that you're a sucker.... But I'm warning you, Princeton. Leave that girl alone." Clenching my fists as I tried to fight my anger off, I remained silent. In my head though, I was going off. Instead of snapping and cursing my dad out like I would've done when I was a teenager, I stood up, adjusted my suit and walked to the door. I definitely made sure I had the last word though and turned around right as I approached the door.

"Just so you know, Kingston..." I emphasized,

talking to him like I did when we were in business meetings, as if we were actual partners and not father and son. "I'm an adult and I'm not going to allow anyone to tell me who I can and cannot talk to. If you don't want me to talk to her, I dare you to try and stop me."

Chapter Three

"SAVE ME FROM YOUR PROMISES."

PEYTON TAHJ EVER.

Because Prince had paid for my room, he automatically had a key. That's why I was surprised to see him at the door. But my racing heart didn't subside. As a matter of fact, smelling his cologne only made it pound harder. When he walked past me, I remained quiet even when he turned around and did a double-take of me. I guess he was expecting me to still look like the scared, vulnerable Peyton he met on the bus. But after one hell of a nap, some food and a hot shower without Shondell breathing down my back about I paid for nothing around her house to be taking showers like a was a queen, I felt like the old invincible Peyton again.

"You smell good." He complimented, sitting next to the bed as he picked up Taylen. I know it was strange for me to allow him to be so close to my baby but for some reason, Princeton made me feel safe. Being around him made me feel like with me and Taylen around him, nothing bad could happen to us. But after watching him leave the hotel room and reminding myself about who that man was, I knew there was no way this was anything minus a little charity towards a broke girl with a baby. I had nothing to offer him, therefore all of this was a waste of time. But still, I sat there and watched Princeton hold and talk to Taylen as if she was his own. I sat there and mourned. For the fact that my daughter would never know the love that her daddy had for her, even though he knew nothing about her before he died. Princeton must have saw that I was in deep thought about something and spoke up, breaking the awkward silence. "Can I ask you a question?"

Feeling a lump gather in my throat, I nodded my head and quickly regretted my decision when I saw him stall. I could tell it was bad news. "Where's Taylen's father? He's not around?" Though I was reminded of Talon's tragedy every day because I wore him around my neck, sometimes I could still feel him around me. But still, thinking about why he wasn't here any more caused a knot to collect in my chest and tug at my heart. I debated on telling Princeton the truth but figuring that after his business trip was over, I'd never see him again, I sucked it up.

"Talon, my daughter's dad, he died before my baby was born. He died before I even knew I was pregnant... He was involved in a serious accident that left him paralyzed from his waist down and was crossing the crosswalk. I guess the driver didn't see him because of the wheelchair, but when I turned around…. His wheelchair was under the bus and he was thrown into oncoming traffic. He survived, I mean he made it… for four whole days afterwards, but he had no brain activity and seeing him laying there lifeless, I knew he wouldn't want to live like that. So I had them pull the plug…" Reminiscing on the worst day of my life, I fought back tears… hard. In my mind, crying was still a sign of weakness. "His mom never forgave me for that either."

"How did you get permission to do that? Pull the plug, I mean? Don't you have to be a relative?" He asked, finally looking up from Taylen.

"Yeah… a blood relative or a spouse." I explained, dropping the ball that nobody else knew. When Talon was killed, we were leaving the courthouse from filing for our marriage license. We'd known it in secret because we knew his mom wouldn't have agreed. She didn't even like me. I knew that there would be more questions about my short, but genuine, marriage to Talon but I was no longer in the mood to talk about him. "A week later, I found out I was more than three months pregnant and had never even had an idea… Five months later, actually five months to the date that her dad died, Taylen Ella-Tahj Ever was born."

"Ever? She only has your last name?" I nodded, and

THE LOVE WE HAD

once again got a bad taste in my mouth over Shondell and her childish antics.

"His mom acted a complete fool in the hospital. While I was trying to have this baby… she was cursing at me, screaming and calling me all kinds of names about how she refused to allow me to give Taylen her father's last name without a DNA test. I was going to name her Tate, but I knew that she had to honor her dad's name somehow, so I named her Taylen Ella, after him… I added Tahj so that a piece of my family name will be with her always. Even when she gets married. Just a few days ago, before I left, the results came back and told her what I knew all along. I heard her, the night I left talking about how she was going to take my baby. *Nobody* is taking my baby from me." I didn't say any more, but by the look on Prince's face, I didn't need to. He knew exactly what I meant and cradled Taylen closet to him, rocking her as she began to flail her arms and legs. The 20-something hour drive he'd spent with us must have embedded itself into his brain because he immediately put her down and got up. I watched him, impressed as hell, as he quickly made her a bottle and then tested it on his skin before giving it to her. She greedily gulped it down, looking just like her damn daddy and I crossed my arms, waiting for him to look up at me but he was too entranced with Taylen.

"Are you sure you don't have any kids?" I asked, sucking my teeth. When he first told me, I believed him. But now, something was up. I just knew it. He was way too good with my baby to not have at least four baby mamas. Looking up at me and meeting my gaze, he must've realized what I was thinking and started to laugh.

"No. I'm sure. The woman that I start my family with, has to have my last name. I refuse to do it any other way." He explained, and I couldn't even about to lie to you. My heart melted when he said that. "But my baby sister Kyra, she had my niece in high school and so she could finish, I'd keep the baby throughout the week and sometimes during the weekend. Kylani, is my goddaughter and she still spends every weekend at Uncle PJ's house. I love that little girl like she's mine... and nobody could tell me that she's not."

He didn't say anything else about it, but I watched as he made faces at Taylen. When he stuck his tongue out at her, I laughed. Not because his face looked funny but because immediately, she tried to do it too. I know that it was wrong to allow my daughter to form a connection with this man, knowing we wouldn't be around long, but it was cute to watch. That's when his phone went off and he stared at it, his complete face changing.

"What is it? What's wrong?" I questioned after he

remained silent for a moment. He dropped his head and I knew it wasn't my place to say anything, so I shut up and waited for him to speak up.

"I have to go home first thing in the morning. Come with me." He offered as my eyes almost bulged out of my head. Yeah sure, I was desperate. But not like that. But just by the look on his face, I could tell he was never going to accept no as a plausible answer. So instead of reminding him about reality, I just shrugged my head and nodded. The smile on his face slowly ate at my heart. If only Princeton knew the truth.

I'd be gone before he woke up in the morning anyways. Closing my eyes, I let silence entrance the room and just when I was about to speak up, I looked at Princeton to find he was sleeping soundly. There was no time better than the present, so I eased off the bed, freezing in my steps when the bed began to creak. Princeton moved, but he didn't wake up so when I noticed his eyes still closed, I sent a silent prayer of thanks up to the heavens. Taylen was sleeping as well so moving as fast as I could to get her dressed, I made sure to keep the pacifier in her mouth so that she wouldn't make a peep. I had become a professional and in less than ten minutes, we were heading out of the hotel like thieves in the night. I didn't know it yet, but running away from Princeton was pointless.

Chapter Four

"WASTING MY TIME ON MY OWN."

PRINCETON JAMES PARRISH.

Six months later...

180 days is a long time to not be able to get someone out of your head but even now, Peyton was haunting my every thought. *What was she doing? Who was she with? Was she safe?* After waking up that next morning and seeing her, her baby, and everything I bought them gone, I just knew what my dad said was true. I had been nothing but an easy solution to the problem she was having. Had it not been me, it would have been some other clueless nigga. At least that's what I told myself. But after having gone down to the customer service desk and reading the note that she's left for me; I knew what the true issue was. In her mind, I was some big shot and she was a handout, unable to do anything. That couldn't have been further from the truth but since she didn't bother to stick around and find out, I was forced to move on with my life... without Peyton. It worked for awhile. I just buried myself deep in work... and in Jersey, hoping for a temporary solution. That only worked for a short time... right up until I called her Peyton's name during sex.

Understandably, that's when things between us two changed, and I knew that it would never be the same. Though I had never crossed the line with Peyton physically, I'd done something much worse. Peyton had affected my mind and my spirit, and now my heart was in another place. Justice did the right thing and called our wedding off.

Now being back in Cleveland, those same bittersweet memories came back like a raging hurricane, but I just sucked it up, reminding myself that this was for the betterment of my future. If this deal went through, not only would it triple my yearly salary, it would leave my future children good for the rest of their lives. The only thing was that it involved a temporary move to Cleveland, which I knew that would heighten my chances of running into Peyton. If she was still here.

When our driver pulled in front of the conference center and let us out, I felt my stomach start turning into knots. Besides this being the biggest deal of my career, and possibly my life, I hadn't been getting much sleep and that left me more in tune with my nervousness than I usually was. For the past few days, I'd been having detailed, explicit dreams of Peyton and I together that usually left me up and haunted, unable to sleep. How I craved a woman that I'd never experienced, I guess I'd never know. But I did. I was. Every time I closed my eyes, I could practically feel her body under mine as we went at it like jackrabbits. The fact that my father booked my brother and I in the Westin didn't help matters either.

Stepping into the La Villa conference center, I waited for KJ to exit the limo as we both walked into the elevator together. Usually I would just attend one of these meetings with my father, but he was off doing something else. Or someone else. It was no secret that my father was unfaithful while my mother was well. Now that she was sick, things didn't get any better. Instead of staying home and tending to his wife, my dad hired someone to care for her during the day, while he did his thing. That's why he ordered KJ to come and act as chief executive of public relations. Even with the non-disclosure agreement we asked everyone to sign, it was clear that someone had slipped up. I could tell that because there were paparazzi outside waiting for us. When we stepped off the elevator, I was oblivious to everything going on around me as I held my breath and prepared to go in here and bullshit the pants off these white people.

In the midst of everything, I must have lost my mind because I was oblivious to the situation around me. But when I looked up, *she* was right there. I didn't even notice her until I heard her voice. Peyton was still just as beautiful as she was six months ago. The only difference was that now she was a little thicker, in all the right places, and the glow on her face had me thinking someone else was involved.

When our eyes met, I could practically see her heart thumping out of her chest. Instead of coming straight to me, Peyton did a complete 360 turn and went the opposite way. Had I been on a personal visit, I would have chased after her. But I needed this mullah so I adjusted my suit and continued to strut to the office with my brother leading the way. The secretary stepped out and then came back carrying two cups of coffee, which we gladly accepted. Minutes passed and just as I was about to check to see if we were early or something, Kingston and I looked up from our phones and quickly put them away, just like our father had taught us when we heard the door open.

I was shocked to see Peyton standing there, but she played it off cool.

"Sorry about that. I'm Peyton Ever." She introduced and when I looked at Kingston, his eyes were bulging out of his head, probably immediately recognizing her name. That's when he stood up and extended his hand.

"I'm Kingston Parrish, Jr. I'm Princeton's brother. It is a pleasure to meet you." He introduced himself and then he sat back down. That's when Peyton's boss, Corie Bradford, walked in. Since that was who we were arranging to see,

Kingston's and I both stood to our feet this time and introduced ourselves. I could tell that she was intrigued by what we had to say from jump, so I played it cool. By the end of my proposal, I could tell she was all for it. While this deal was what I had been looking forward to for months, the entire time I was giving my speech, I couldn't even get my mind off Peyton. I even managed to steal a few glances at her, just to see that she had already been looking at me.

Clearing my throat to let her know I was finished speaking, I waited as she clapped her hands.

"Very impressive, Mr. Parrish. We'd like to get started with this deal immediately. Peyton has written up the required documents so if you'd like to look over-," That's when my brother chimed in.

"Actually, that's my job." When Peyton passed the papers over to him, I watched KJ's demeanor change as he carefully analyzed every piece of the article. When he nodded his head and approved it, he passed it over to me. I read it over once again and then we both pulled out pens and signed our names.

"I do have one concern though." I interjected after passing the documents back to Peyton. "We required that all of your staff sign a non-disclosure agreement. Someone broke that. There are paparazzi-." That's when Peyton interjected, clearing her throat.

"That is why we were late, Mr. Parrish. Our leak was identified and exterminated from our team. Breeches in our system will not be tolerated." She spoke firmly. Making sure we were both on the same page, I looked at my brother and it was clear that he was just as impressed as I was.

"Do you have artists in mind?" KJ asked. I watched as Peyton's face started to glow as she proudly sat up.

"We've decided to throw a fundraiser, a talent show." Corie spoke. Knowing that this was the kind of exposure our team needed, I nodded to KJ and he pulled out the checkbook. When Peyton and Corie saw what we were offering, their jaws dropped. When his part of the job he was done, KJ excused himself to go cure himself from his ailing hangover and Peyton's boss left to go take a conference call. That left Peyton and I in the room together, alone and I immediately stood up.

"Where did you go, Peyton? Why did you leave me like that?" I asked, unable to filter the questions before they flew out of my mouth. She sighed sadly and I could see her bottom lip trembling, but that didn't stop me from wanting my answers. She couldn't cry her way out of this one. Peyton still wasn't talking, but I wasn't giving up. "I would have given you the world." That seemed to get her attention and she looked up, tears welling up in her eyes.

"Exactly and what could I give you, Prince? Nothing. I'm no good for you. I'm a single mom. I just got a decent job and I am barely making a way out of no way, right now." She confessed. Checking the clock, she cursed under her breath. "Fuck, I'm going to be late to get Taylen from daycare." She mumbled, rushing out, I assumed to get in her car. For some reason I did the creepiest thing possible and followed her. When she saw me, she turned around.

"Can I see Taylen sometime this week? I miss her." I confessed. That wasn't a lie. What I didn't say was that while I missed Taylen, I missed Peyton way more. Nervously biting on her lip, I watched Peyton think about it before nodding.

"If you want, you can come with me to get her." Following closely behind her, I was too busy watching her apple-shaped ass jiggle beneath her skirt to pay attention but when she unlocked her car, I immediately felt how proud she was as she grinned at me.

"I see you! Riding in a foreign..." I complimented her as she pretended to bow and got in the car. I followed suit and got in the passenger's side. The ride was quick. I wasn't sure if it was because Peyton was driving like she was trying to kill us both or because I spent the entire ride listening to her sing and laughing, but either way, we were pulling into

Taylen's daycare before I knew what was happening.

Walking inside, I smiled as I watched all of these kids' parents pick them up. On one hand, I was extremely excited to see Taylen again. I knew there was no possibility of her remembering me, but that didn't stop me. I couldn't help but wonder if she was crawling yet, or if she'd even allow me to hold her. I could feel the heat from Peyton's hands since they were only millimeters away from me but knowing that she had a habit of running when she got overwhelmed, I refrained from reaching out and grabbing it.

Just as I started to get antsy, an older woman came out carrying Taylen as she slept. Peyton laughed and grabbed her, but then she woke up and I watched as her eyes focused in on me. Her stare was intense, especially to be just a baby. I thought she was about to cry because I saw her lips start quivering, but then I laughed as she started to smile and then reached out for me.

"You have to be Taylen's father... I've never seen her do that with anyone." The older woman interjected as I tried to suppress a nervous coughing fit. Grabbing Taylen from Peyton, I shrugged the woman's comments off.

"Nah, I'm not her father. I'm just a man who loves her and her mother very much..." The correction seemed to shut her up and as I glanced at Peyton, it didn't look like she had anything to say either. Tickling Taylen, she squealed

THE LOVE WE HAD

loudly as we all headed out and back into the car. I could tell that she was surprised that I knew how to strap the baby in, but like I said before, even though I didn't have kids of my own, I wasn't new to this. Besides, putting a baby in a carseat only took a little bit of common sense.

I got back in the passenger's seat and Peyton started the car up. I could tell something was on her mind but I didn't want to push it, so I remained quiet while I waited for her to speak up. Eventually, she did.

"Would you like to have dinner with me? With us?" Peyton offered and I shifted uncomfortably in my seat. In my mind, nothing in the world would be better than to share a meal with Peyton but I was afraid of going too far and having Peyton as my meal instead. That kind of an unwanted advance could kill this deal before the ink even dried. I was reluctantant, but willing so I nodded my head. I didn't even need to look at Peyton to realize she was smiling from ear to ear. When we pulled into her house after a fifteen or twenty-minute drive, she practically skipped out of her car, grabbed Taylen and then we headed inside of her apartment. The moment that I walked in, I was impressed as hell. I knew situations where it took people a year, or more, to get back on their feet after something. But after what Peyton had gone through, she managed to get on her feet in no time. It looked like she was doing well for herself. Directing me to sit on the couch, Peyton put Taylen in my arms again and walked off to the kitchen. I watched Taylen laugh and giggle, I stared at her in awe. It was hard to believe that I was holding the same baby that slept in my lap during a 25-hour bus ride six months ago, but she was.

Then something crazy happened. The moment that Peyton walked back in to the living room to give me a glass of water, Taylen grabbed me by my ears and gave me a kiss, leaving drool all over my face. I didn't mind it and quickly kissed her on the cheek, watching as she laughed hysterically. I was used to my niece kissing me, so I pulled her away and tickled the area under her chin. I looked up just in time to see Peyton staring at me and Taylen with tears in her eyes. "She's never done that before. Not even to me." I didn't want to over-step boundaries, especially knowing how mothers got when it came to their babies' firsts. I tried to pass Taylen back, but she started to scream. Apparently, she didn't want to leave my arms. "No, no. It's okay, Prince. I'm fine." Peyton stopped me, quickly wiping her tears. She probably noticed the worry written all over my face. "She probably remembers your smell." She added, walking back into the kitchen. Since I had read somewhere that babies grew attached to scents before they ever even recognized faces, Peyton's answer made a lot of sense. Taylen was on my shoulder cooing but after awhile, I didn't feel her moving around anymore. She even stopped babbling and cooing which let me know that she was sleeping. I wanted to put her down so that I could talk to Peyton but she had a football player's grip on the collar of my shirt.

I walked into the kitchen where Peyton was cooking dinner and started to laugh.

"Damn, she must have really missed me." Peyton laughed as well and then took her baby out of my arms and put her in the back room. When she emerged, she made two plates and then we both sat down on the couch. Peyton turned on the TV and we ate quietly. Minutes passed and the silence was starting to get uncomfortable. At least, for me.

"Yeah. I guess we both did…" Glancing at her out of the corner of my eye, Peyton's eyes never left the TV. *Maybe she hadn't even meant for those words to come out of her mouth.* If she was hoping I would drop it and change the subject though, she had me mixed up with another nigga. Her leaving so abruptly was still a sore spot for me.

"You left me. Not the other way around. Remember?" I snapped, my words coming out harsher than I anticipated for them to. Even Peyton seemed surprised with me. But she still stayed calm. After awhile, she nodded her head and seemed to be figuring it out in her own mind. Pointing to her apartment, I motioned around so that she could see how upset I really was. "I was willing to give you this, Pey-," I started to explain, before she began waving her hands around like a crazy woman and cut me off.

"That's why I left, Princeton! Don't you understand? Don't you get it? I don't want *anyone* to give me anything, because then it can just be taken away from me! I got the job done by myself, didn't I?" she started to yell loudly, which let me know that I'd struck a nerve. Before I could say anything else, she seemed to calm herself down. "You don't get it, Prince. You've never had to do for yourself." She said, pausing as I laughed under my breath. In all honesty, Peyton had no idea about what I had to do in order to get where I was now. "I am so tired of people saying I wouldn't have something if it wasn't for them. I just want to walk into my house with my name on the lease... drive around in my car with my name on the title. I worked my ass off to get where I'm at, just so nobody could ever take that from me. Is that so bad? I'm not anybody's charity case." Finally, I could see the point that she was trying to make, so I shut up. For a second anyways.

Figuring there was nothing left to say, I did the only thing I could think of to do. The only thing that I had been thinking about all day. I leaned over and kissed her, despite the fact that I was nervous she wouldn't reciprocate. The last thing I wanted to do was overstep my boundaries. Then I felt her hand gliding over the top of my head and to the back of my neck, pulling me closer and eliminating the very little personal space we both had to begin with. Things got intense quickly but knocking at the door interrupted us. Peyton looked like she had seen a ghost. When I looked up and saw a nigga standing there furious, it felt like I had too.

He sat his keychain on the counter and I immediately stood up as I prepared to fight. I hadn't been involved in a brawl since high school, but ol' dude looked like he wanted to knock my head into the wall, so I was ready for whatever. People always confused me with some soft nigga. But just because I was a businessman, it didn't mean I was a pussy. Peyton must have sensed it too because she walked over to him and I prepared myself to hear her lie. I immediately figured she was about to pick him over me, so I knew it was time to bounce. I prepared my things, getting ready to remove myself from this messy situation. But then she surprised me. "You don't need to leave, Prince." She stopped me as she faced the man who walked into her house. I'm not even about to lie. I was tuned into that shit like a Cavs game, because I wanted to know what was going to happen next. "Blake, I really like you… I do, but you've known for awhile that this wasn't going to work out. You don't excite me…

you barely acknowledge my daughter. This can't continue. As a woman, as a mother, we have to end this. I'm sorry." To watch Peyton's old flame get his heart broken like that was painful, especially since Peyton was so nonchalant about it. The fact that she was so cold and smooth about it had me side-eyeing her, but I kept my mouth shut as Blake's eyes darted between both of us. At the same time, I was relieved that she was basically letting me know that I had no competition.

"So you cheat on me with this dude and now, I'm the one that's faulty? Fuck you, Peyton." He grabbed his keys and headed toward the door, but Peyton called out to him and stopped him in his tracks. His face looked so hopeful that she had changed her mind, but I could tell that wasn't it.

"I need my key back." Like a bitch, Blake pulled the key off the ring and threw it right at Peyton. It barely missed her face and that's when I stepped forward.

"She already told you it's time for you to leave… Don't add insult to injury and catch an assault charge too." I tried to show him that he really didn't want that problem, but the closer I got to him, I could see the anger in his eyes. Then just like that, he started to laugh and backed away, heading to the door.

"Be careful. You see how she did me. She'll do the same thing to you." He chuckled, heading to the door. This time, it was my turn to laugh. It was clear he didn't know me or the history behind Peyton and I. All I needed was a little time, and Blake would no longer be at the forefront of Peyton's mind.

Chapter Five

"NO ONE SEES WHAT I SEE IN YOU."

PEYTON TAHJ EVER.

Turning back around toward Princeton, I almost broke into hysteria when I saw his face. "What?" I couldn't help but smile seeing the confused look on his face.

"Are you good... I mean, like you need some time or something?" Prince asked me sheepishly. For the first time ever, Princeton James Parrish was visibly nervous as his eyes jetted from me, to the door, and then back again. Just to calm him down, I went and locked it even though I knew nothing was about to go down. Blake wasn't even like that.

"What would I need time for? I'm good." Responding quickly, I sat him on the couch and then went into the refrigerator as I searched for my stress relief. Pulling two bottles out of there, I went and held them up. "White or red?" Holding up both bottles, I watched as he tried to quickly make his mind up.

"Peyton, after what just happened... I'm going to need something a little stronger than that." I couldn't help but laugh and went back to the kitchen and came back with Hennessy and patron.

"Better?" I asked.

"How did you even get those? You're not 21." He asked, as I shot him a look that asked him if he really wanted to know. In return, he shrugged and we moved on. I knew that he was probably very surprised that I was so cold-hearted with Blake, but this wasn't about him any more. I was trying to be on my Netflix and chill with him.

"Princeton, stop looking at me like that I really did miss you and felt the connection from the first day I met you on the bus. I was just tired of people saying they helped me, just to be able to say they did and throw it back in my face. As far as Blake goes, he was really just something to do. We didn't have a connection and my daughter didn't fuck with him. She cried just by him looking at her. Any mother knows that is a red flag. Besides, she showed me today who she missed and who has a special place in her heart. Now can we please sit down watch some movies, drink, talk and catch up?" With a slick smirk on his face, Princeton gave me the smile that instantly made me wet.

"Okay, Peyton. I'll take a shot of Hennessy. But if boy come back tripping, I can't be held responsible for my actions." We sat down and started flipping through what Netflix had, but nothing was really catching our eyes. "Do you have cards?"

"Yea I do. Why?"

"Let's play black deuce for shots." I didn't really know what that was but after he walked me through it, it seemed easy enough.

I went and grabbed the deck of cards and we started to play. About seven hands in, he had three shots and I had four. I could feel the liquor taking over and what Princeton didn't know was that Hennessy made me so horny. I chuckled to myself as I scolded myself for not sticking with Patron. At least I could handle that. As we sat there laughing and talking, I decided that we should switch the game up a little bit and play Strip black deuce instead. I didn't want to keep playing for shots and ruin the night throwing up. Besides, a massive hangover and having Taylen to take care of wasn't going to work. Of course, Princeton quickly agreed but only under one condition; we got to pick the piece of clothing the other had to take off.

He won the first game, and I laughed because I instantly knew I had set myself up to be naked. "Peyton, baby take that shirt off." I jokingly rolled my eyes and took my shirt off, watching as his eyes roamed my body and clearly approving of what he saw. I had been working out, so I already knew my stomach was flat & titties were sitting up looking good in my red lace bra.

That first win must have been ammunition and the motivation he needed because he quickly won again and ordered me out of my leggings. I had the matching lace panties on, so I knew this was going lead to trouble. Before I could sit back down, Princeton was up and in my face. The look he was giving me had my pussy instantly getting wet. I wanted him in the worst way. Princeton took his shirt and pants off and I put my cards down, knowing the game was now over. However, the playing had just started. Princeton's body was to die for. He had a six-pack with that sexy ass v-cut. My hands traced down his chest and I could see the top of his polo boxers, where I could already see that monster of a dick print. I unbuckled his pants for him, so he knew that it was time to stop playing. I wanted all of him. He stopped me, picked me up and pinned me up against the wall. When we started kissing, I could feel him unsnapping my bra. First, he started to leave gentle, clean kisses on my neck, right behind my ear.

"Damn, Princeton..." I murmured. He started to sucked on my titties so gently. Then he nibbled on them and a moan escaped my mouth. "Princeton, baby...I need to feel you inside me now." I whined. He didn't say nothing but carried me over to the couch and laid me down. Ripping off my panties and instantly started back with those damn kisses on the inside of my thighs. "Princeton, baby..."

"What's up, baby? What's wrong?" Before I could respond, he attacked my clit and my words got caught in my throat.

"Princeton, fuck!"

"Baby, you taste so good..." he whispered, the vibration of his words rocking their way across my clit.

"Princeton!" I started to scream out his name as I was cumming. He didn't stop, as a matter of fact, he just kept eating and sucking like he wanted every drop of it. He put two fingers inside of me and I started feeling something I had never felt before. "Princeton baby, get up... I have to pee." I tried pushing his head away, but he was entirely too strong for me. He laughed and shook his head, his nose rubbing up against my clit as I slowly felt myself losing my mind.

"Nah baby, you're not about to pee... you're about to squirt. Give me that...when you feel it again, let it go." He instructed me, going right back to what he was doing before. I listened to him and as that feeling came back, I let go and squirted all over him. He caught majority of it and I laid there, in shock and out of breath. I couldn't feel my legs, so I knew there was no way I was going anywhere for awhile.

The moment that my eyes fluttered open, I found myself confused as hell. It was still dark outside, so the only thing that I could make out was the fluorescent outline of the numbers on the clock. That's when it suddenly hit me and I hopped out of bed, not thinking about anything except for that I'd been sleep for over seven hours and hadn't heard Taylen cry once. I finally rose to my feet and as the blood traveled to my toes, the explicit but delightful memories of the night before flooded to my brain. With each step I took, my thighs burned as if Princeton had branded his name onto them. Still, I feverishly ran from one room to the next, looking for any sign of Prince and my daughter. I was just about to freak out when I spotted Princeton sprawled out across the couch with Taylen fast asleep on his chest. He must have heard my footsteps because when he turned his head towards me, he immediately put his finger to his lips as if I would risk waking up my own baby.

"She's been like that all night?" I asked, astounded. Taylen never slept so soundly on someone's chest. Not even mine. I was surprised that Prince didn't wake up with a baby toe in his mouth honestly.

"Nah, not the whole night. *We* were together the entire night. I heard her starting to wake up and I didn't want her to wake you up, so I gave her a bottle, changed her diaper and she kinda sort of just fell right back to sleep." I watched as he looked down at her and started to pat her back when she stirred. When her eyes started to open, I sighed and went to take Taylen from his arms, but he showed me away. But I was reluctant. The last thing I wanted was for a nigga to feel obligated to hold mine constantly. On the other hand, I was pretty convinced that Princeton cared for Taylen more than he cared for me and that made me happy. Instead of getting annoyed that he refused to give me my baby back, I watched intensely as he hummed some secret song that immediately got her right back to sleep.

I guess with me being awake finally, Princeton had something else on his mind so he placed my baby in her bassinet and then grabbed me by the hand as we left the living room together. Sitting him behind the island in my kitchen, I took out everything from my refrigerator that I wanted to cook for him and for the first time in a long time, I actually stopped to think about how far I had come. Six months ago, I had no idea where my next meal was going to come from or where my daughter and I were going to lay our heads. The very next day, I got accepted into a transitional housing shelter and soon after, I found a job that allowed me to get my own place.

I started to chop vegetables up for an omelette, but it seemed Princeton had other plans. Picking my entire body, he placed me on the counter and put his hand over my mouth as he stripped me out of my clothes, throwing them all to his feet. He was calm, yet so feverish that his plans scared me, but I went with the flow anyways.

"You're not hungry?" I croaked, my voice cracking as I tried to stifle a moan. I could feel my breathing becoming constructed as he started to trail his way across my clavicle with his tongue. Yes, we'd had sex before but that was when I'd had some liquid courage. Now I'd had none and it seemed that the old me, the inexperienced, nervous me was back.

"I am… but what I have a taste for, you can't make.

It's between your thighs." Just as he was about to go down on me, I heard banging on the door and someone yelling outside of my apartment. It was definitely a female's voice, someone I didn't recognize, and she was calling for Princeton to come outside. I wanted to go check it out regardless, but he seemed to ignore it, intent on tasting me until Taylen woke up screaming her poor little lungs out. I went to go put her back to sleep and Princeton went to the door, to figure out things with that female by himself. I could hear them talking from my baby's nursery but the nosiness in me made me put her in her crib so I could really see what was going on. Once the woman on my front stairs saw me, she started going in. Maybe girls from Princeton's past would have tolerated it, but I wasn't that one.

"Damn, PJ. You move on quick, don't you?" She snarled, looking me up and down. A year ago, I would've covered myself but to be honest, I knew I was the shit now. I'd lost weight but gained it back in the right places, and my skin was glowing and popping. "And you sure do downgrade, too. What is she? Seventeen? You're messing with minors now?" She snapped. Before I could even control or censor the words coming out of my mouth, I stepped forward and prepared to show this lady why I wasn't the one to play with.

"No, bitch…. Actually I'm about to be nineteen, with

my own spot. I have a car with no car note and my refrigerator is stacked. You pulled up to my place. Therefore, the only downgrade I see is that beat up bucket in my driveway. So move it and leave, before I have you towed. You look like a psycho." I threatened. I couldn't help the chuckle that escaped my mouth when I noticed the crazy look on her face. She looked like she was ready to lunge at me.

"Whatever," she responded, waving me off as if she didn't care. I could tell by the look on her face that I'd gotten under her skin though. "You're just temporary anyways. Princeton is mine. He will always be mine." She said as if I cared. That's when Princeton finally interjected and interrupted our back and forth argument and spoke up.

"Jersey, you shouldn't be here. Don't do this to yourself. It's over between us... I belong with Peyton." He spoke finally, leaving no room for question or debates. I stood there with my arms crossed over my chest, enjoying the scene unfolding in front of me. Not the fact that a woman was getting her heart broken because I had been there and done that before. However, it didn't seem like Jersey was willing to let it go that easily and grabbed his hands, trying to unsuccessfully pull him to her. That's when I stepped in and shut all of that down.

"I'm not sure if you can hear me or not, but I believe

he said that you shouldn't be here. That means leave. Go. Bye." I interrupted, the most wicked smile on my face. She seemed to be turning around and heading down the driveway, but then she spun back around and spit on me. Princeton was fast, but I was faster so I quickly jumped on ol' girl. Weaving her hair in between my hands, I punched her mercilessly over and over again until my hands pulsed and my knuckles swelled. I could hear her screaming for Prince to get me off of her and though he was trying, I was not letting go of her until I proved my point.

Eventually, I got tired and let up. That was the only reason Princeton was able to lift me off of her and fling me into the house like a ragdoll. I wasn't interested in beating on the girl any more because for one, I was tired. For two, the last thing I wanted was the police called to my door. I had just got my life on track and my job was too important for me to lose over some silly, obsessed woman. For a second when I heard him talking to her, my insecurities got the best of me and I swore he was about to choose up with her.

"What the hell were you thinking, Jersey? That's what we're doing now? You showed up at her house and spit on her!! You're lucky she didn't beat your ass and call the cops on you for assault." He scolded her. That's when his voice dropped a couple of octaves and I listened closely. "I've moved on, Jers. You need to, too." That's when she began laughing again. I had half a mind to go out there and stomp on her head, but instead I gave Princeton the time he needed to diffuse the situation and get her away from my house.

"Why do you want that young ass girl, anyways? She can't do what I do for you. She can't make you feel like I do." I heard her say, right before Princeton stepped in and cut her off.

"She's Peyton. *The* Peyton." He informed her. She must've realized that she would never win the fight because she sadly dropped her head and walked away. I'd been the broken-hearted girl before so that's why I chose not to relish in her misery. God knows I wanted to, though. Especially with all that mess she was talking.

When Prince walked back in, he ran his hands over his face like the whole situation had stressed him out and I almost wanted to laugh, but I didn't want to give him the satisfaction of knowing I wasn't mad about it. Not yet, at least. So I washed some dishes out and pretended he didn't exist. When he pulled me closer to him by my wrists, I didn't even fight back. I couldn't. Instead, I melted into him like a chocolate kiss sitting outside on a hot day.

"How does she know where I live, Prince? Where me and my baby lay our heads at night? And what did you mean by I'm Peyton? She doesn't know me." I questioned, letting him know that I'd overheard their conversation. I watched his face change and prepared for him to start lying to me. I just knew it was coming. But then he did something unexpected, grabbing me by the hand and leading me to the couch. He sat down and then pulled me on to his lap so that I was straddling him. He placed his head on my chest and listened to my heartbeat, remaining quiet for a moment. I could feel his chest rising and falling, but I didn't want to repeat my question hastily. So I waited.

"She saw my car in the driveway. That's how she knew I was here…. And as far as her knowing who you were, she didn't know your face. But she definitely knew your name. I blurted it out. That's why our engagement was called off, because she swore I was cheating. But I promise you Peyton, I would never put you in any situation that would hurt you or Taylen. If you think that I had something to do with her coming here, you're absolutely wrong. All I want is for you and your daughter to be healthy, happy and safe."

Thought I knew he thought his response had shut me up, and it had, it was only because I couldn't think of anything else to say. That's when Prince took the initiative to lift his head up and kiss me. Really kiss me. I was about to strip him out of his clothes, but then my phone started ringing like crazy. Princeton felt me trying to get up, but held me down by my waist as he attacked my neck with fervent, passionate kisses. The lower he went, the more I imagined him kissing me the same way on my second set of lips.

The phone wouldn't stop ringing and it was starting to piss me off, so I answered it while relishing in the feeling of his lips all my exposed flesh.

"Hello?" I half-moaned, running my fingers through his hair. I wasn't sure if I wanted him further from me or closer to me, but it was hard to concentrate and remember that I was on the phone. Princeton was driving me crazy. "Hello?" I asked again. I was pretty sure, at this point, that nobody was on the other line. When I looked at the screen and saw that there was someone calling me blocked, I immediately got a sinking feeling in my stomach. I quickly ended the call and left it alone, but then I got an alert that I had a voicemail.

Chapter Six

"WOULD YOU BE HONEST, BABY?"

SHONDAE LATRELLE MASON.

I watched as my mom paced back and forth, talking to whomever that was don the phone. I could tell by the look on her face that whatever she was up to was no good, but I would have had to been crazy to speak up against her, especially to her face. Whatever she was doing, as long as she kept me out of it, I'd be okay.

"Are you sure that it's her? Are you sure it's Peyton?" Hearing the name of the girl that gave my big brother his first and only child, I immediately invested myself into her conversation. No matter what Peyton believed, I had never had anything against her. Unfortunately though, because I was only sixteen, there wasn't much I could do. My mom was the only person who ever hated seeing them together. My dad agreed with me, that Peyton was a very respectful young lady and from what I'd seen, she seemed to be taking care of my niece very well. I'd never told my mom but I used my friend's page to sometimes sneak and take a glance at

Taylen. She was turning out to look just like my brother. My mom's hate for Peyton though stemmed from a different issue, but that was a different story for a different day. I took a peek at what my mom was looking at and the picture was clearly Peyton. I winced at the bought of what she planned to do next. When she felt it was necessary, Shondell, my mother, could be wicked and conniving. "Yes, yes. I'll be in touch first thing in the morning. I need to make the proper arrangements." After hanging up the phone, my mom began to stare off into space but I didn't even go need to glance in that direction to know what she was looking at.

On top of our credenza, my mom had built a shrine in Talon's memory. Pictures of us together when I was a baby, and overdramatized family portraits adorned the whole top level. In an act of spite after my brother's death, my mom cropped Peyton out of all of Talon's pictures. It wasn't right, but it also wasn't anything new to me. From the very beginning of their relationship, my mom despised Peyton. The volatile relationship she and my mom shared only intensified after Taylen was born. I never once blamed her for taking the baby away from our toxic living situation. With Talon gone, my mom felt free to say and do whatever she wanted, with nobody to tell her she was overstepping her boundaries any more.

"Why can't you just leave Peyton alone? She's doing well... and she's taking care of Taylen. That's all that matters, right?" I asked innocently. The moment the words came out of my mouth though, I knew that I had messed up. My mom's death glare instantly shut me up. If you were raised by a black woman, you know the exact look I'm talking about.

"Do you realize how foolish you sound? That little girl is the last piece of my only baby that I have left," she snapped as I ignored the stinging in my eyes. I'd jump in front of a train before I ever let my mom see me cry. It wasn't like her idolizing Talon was anything new. For as long as I could remember, my mom's whole life revolved around Talon Elliot Mason. Especially after our dad left and married someone else, leaving my brother as "man of the house." Now, even with him gone, it was like nothing had changed. It still seemed as though I was invisible, only able to be seen when it involved doing something that benefited Shondell. "Now, if I have to pry Taylen from Peyton's cold, dead arms, then that's just what will have to happen. I told Talon, I told him! I never liked that girl. I told him that she was no good and that she was a user, but look at him now! He's dead and Peyton is out living her life! But now.... Now, my grandbaby is here and I have no intention of letting that sneaky, ratchet bitch raise her."

THE LOVE WE HAD

Staying silent, I kept to myself since I didn't want my mom to unleash her wrath out on me. That didn't mean I was going to stand idly by though. I knew exactly how to get her to shut the hell up and chill out. I poured her a cup of tea and sneakily smashed up two sleeping pills, adding them and then stirring quickly so it would dissolve and not be stuck to the bottom of the cup. Handing the cup over, I watched her sip as she walked to her room and I knew that in less than thirty minutes, she would be out like a light. Watching the little hand make its way around the clock, I counted down like it was New Year's Eve and just like clockwork, I could hear her snoring. When I creeped into her room, drool was cascading its way down her chin and so I quickly snatched up her phone and then made my way into the bathroom. Shutting the door and locking it behind me, I looked through her history until I found the number of the private investigator that she had hired and pressed dial. It was late so I knew there was a chance he wouldn't pick up, but that didn't stop me from holding my breath as the phone rang over and over. Just as I was about to hang up, his husky voice came over the speaker and I knew that I didn't have time to waste, so I disguised my voice as my mom's and lied the best that I could.

"I need the number you called. I want to speak to

Peyton." I requested, whispering like a church mouse and he quickly gave it to me while I wrote it down. Only seconds after hanging up, I was dialing Peyton's number. Something in me told me that she wouldn't answer, but I still let the phone continue to ring, until I got her voicemail. Initially, I wasn't going to leave a message, but I felt like Peyton deserved to know what my mom was planning so I cleared my throat and began to speak. "Hi Peyton... I'm sure you know who this is. I know we have never really been on the best of terms, but this is really important. My mom is up to something. She wants Taylen. You have to call me back." I half-whispered. The last thing I wanted to do was get upset and wake my mom up so I kept my voice down. "Please. Call me back."

Chapter Seven.

MY WORLD'S ON FIRE,"

PRINCETON JAMES PARRISH.

The whole vibe changed when Peyton received that call and I knew that whoever it was, it definitely wasn't somebody that she wanted to talk to. Her entire mood was off, so I sat her down quickly and snatched her phone. When I pressed the button to play the voicemail, I watched Peyton's entire body begin to shake nervously. The longer the woman spoke, the more Peyton's hands started to shake. Eventually, the entire tips of her fingers were damn-near white because of how hard she was squeezing them together. I didn't know who the person was, but it was apparent that Peyton did. However, when I heard the woman talk about taking Taylen, I'd heard enough and quickly called back. I could tell that Peyton wasn't expecting that, but there was no way I was about to sit around and watch this happen. Not when I had the resources to stop it.

"Hello?" someone answered, almost immediately. I didn't care about her name, or any of that. At that moment, I was seeing red and didn't care. Anyone who had something to do with this was about to feel me. Peyton was growing more nervous by the moment, but I grabbed her by the hand so that she would know everything was okay. "Who is this?"

I remembered Peyton telling me their last name when we first met, so I cleared my throat and prepared to make this woman hate her life. I wasn't in the business of talking crazy to a woman old enough to be my mother but Peyton and Taylen were my babies, even if they didn't know it yet, and I was not about to sit around and let anyone tear them apart.

"Hello, Ms. Mason-,"

"Mrs. Mason. My name is Mrs. Mason. Who is this?" she snapped. I had never heard the witch's voice from Hansel and Gretel, but Taylen's grandma's voice was a close second to the scariest voice I'd ever heard in my life. It was like someone had swallowed a toad and then lit their esophagus on fire. The shit was creepy.

"Anyways, the last thing that I called to talk to you about is the pronunciation of your name. I could care less. I just wanted to let you know that my name is

Princeton J. Parrish… My family calls me PJ, but you may recognize me from Parrish & Prince. My father, Kingston Sr., is the CEO and I'm the COO. I'm not sure what kind of impression you're under, but I promise you, Taylen is very well taken care of-,"

"I don't care! I don't care! She belongs with me! I'm her blood! Nobody will take care of her better than me!" Mrs. Mason was now screaming at the top of her lungs and I knew that Peyton could hear her because she started to cry. I put my finger to my lips so that she would quiet down. The last thing I wanted was the old bitch thinking she had the upper-hand. That couldn't have been further from the truth. While she was busy ranting and going off, I was pulling my phone out in order to find a very important number. Once I found it, I dialed it into Peyton's phone and once he answered, I merged the calls.

"And Peyton is her mother. Nobody loves that little girl more than her. I've seen it with my own two eyes." I counter-stated. I didn't want to say anything that would be considered instigating but I was enjoying tormenting the old woman. I was really getting a rise out of her.

Just like I planned, he was quiet the entire time

while Taylen's grandmother was screaming obscenities and threats. All in all, she was eating right out of the palm of my hand and didn't even know it.

"Here's the thing, Mrs. Mason… While I do agree that you have every right to see and visit with your granddaughter, I am only comfortable with it if Peyton is… Since she has made it clear that you will not be a part of Taylen's life, and I can clearly see why, there is no reason for you to try to do something slick. Rod, are you there?" I asked, now chiming in so that my lawyer would know that it was his turn to speak. "If and when she decides to let you see Taylen, I'm all for that. Right now though, it looks like you need to get your act together first. My lawyer, Rod Samuels, here has taken account and is recording every threat and obscenity that you've thrown over the line and I'm sure that this is sufficient reason for a protection order. Isn't it, Rod?" I asked, kissing Peyton on the forehead as a sigh of relief washed over her. Rod began taking over and soon, all we heard was a click, meaning Mrs. Mason had hung up. When the line was clear, Peyton squealed and jumped into my arms, waking Taylen up in the process.

"Tell you what, Peyton… Why don't we get out of here? Me, you, Taylen… Just for a few days. We'll go to Chicago to meet face to face with my lawyer, we'll have a deep dish pizza or two and we'll just relax. Besides, we can't be served with any documents if we're not here." I explained to her my idea and she agreed almost instantly, the fear of losing her child trumping over any and everything else. "Do you have some time off?" That's when Peyton shook her head, and I handed her my phone. "Call your job and tell them you have an emergency. They'll see you again on Wednesday."

"What if I lose my job, Princeton? I can't afford that right now." Now, her mind was starting to fill with doubt. I wasn't having it though and pushed my phone further into her hand.

"Call them... Anything that you lose, will be reimbursed right back to you. I promise you that."

After leaving her job a quick but satisfactory message, we started packing her and Taylen's bags. It only took us a few minutes, because I promised her that whatever we didn't have, I would buy when we made it to our destination. I quickly called up my driver who made it to Peyton's front door in no time, and then we headed off to the airport. Peyton had never been showered with the finer things in life before, so when we made it to the airport, I watched her face as I instructed my driver to drive to the back, where our private jet was waiting for us.

A regular flight from Cleveland to Chicago was about an hour but we made it there in about forty-five minutes, just in time for dinner. As we stepped off the plane, I booked a hotel room for us in a luxurious suite and then we went to go buy some stuff. A bassinet for Taylen came first, though. I wanted Peyton to fully relax on this trip, even if that meant I had to put baby girl in her own room so that I could give her mommy a much needed back-shot. I knew that we were meeting with Rod first thing in the morning, so I wanted tonight to be extra special. I wanted Peyton to not regret choosing me over that lame ass nigga, Blake. He could never do for her what I did, and I'd bet my life on that.

When we finally got settled into our room, and got Taylen's bed set up, I ordered food and Peyton and I laid up and watched TV while we waited for it.

"Why are you doing all of this?" she asked, weaving my finger in between hers. Taylen had a bottle already, so she was in the other room passed out. We wanted to keep it that way, so when the room service knocked on the door heavily, Peyton headed to make sure she was still sleeping and I went to the door so that they wouldn't keep beating like the damn police. I knew they were just doing their job but when I heard Taylen crying, I immediately got agitated and quickly took the trays from the room service worker and shut the door in his face, after giving him a measly and pathetic tip. I lifted the lids and sat the trays on the table as I heard Peyton rocking the baby back to sleep. When I heard a door shut behind me, I looked to see Peyton with her finger to her lips and she didn't have to tell me twice. After hearing Taylen cry pretty much the entire flight, probably because the air pressure was a lot on her ears, the last thing I wanted to do was wake her up. When Peyton saw the food that I ordered, her jaw dropped.

"I'm doing this because I love you, Peyton. I've loved you since I met you and I know it sounds crazy, I know it sounds impossible. But no matter what you think, you're not a charity case to me. You're a woman, a strong, determined woman who has been through a lot but never let it break you. In my eyes, that means you're invincible and nothing can break you. There is nothing more attractive to me than someone whose odds were stacked against them, but you climbed those and you did what you had to do for you and Taylen. You're doing it, Peyton... but you shouldn't have to do it alone. I don't want you to do it alone. Let me be your man. The man that you need in your life." I could tell by the look on her face that she was feeling what I was saying. But I needed more than that. I needed her to feel *me.* So I pulled her in my lap and she placed her hands on my chest. "This is not just a physical connection even though our chemistry is fucking insane, Peyton. My bond to you, your daughter, came way before I even touched you or felt the inside of you." I muttered, my head on her chest as I listened to the way her heart pounded vivaciously. Lifting my head up so that we were looking each other in the eyes, Peyton put her hand on my cheek and stroked my face. The longer we stared at each other, the more intense it became and I could feel my dick starting to rise up. She felt it too, and chuckled as she rose off of me. I surprised her when I held her down by her waist so that she couldn't move. All our clothes were on, yet we were touching like we were fucking and that was fine with me. When our mouths connected, fireworks went off and I know that shit sound cliché as hell, but that's literally what I felt. Her mouth tasted so good, like bubble gum and sprite and I couldn't get enough. "Why you trying to move like you don't know what to do with it? Huh?" I gently gripped her neck and laughed as her heart began to race. She never pulled away and I felt a slight moan come from her throat.

Then just like that, I laid back on the couch and Peyton laid on top of me. I thought something else was about to go down, but I was perfectly content with our heartbeats syncing as we both fell asleep.

"I'm too tired to even eat..." she murmured, and I could tell by how low her voice was getting that she was on her way to sleep.

"It's okay... We have a long day tomorrow. Get some sleep."

Chapter Eight

"HOPING THAT YOU'D COME ALONG,"

KINGSTON COLBY PARRISH, SR.

The one thing that I loved about being in charge was that even when P.J thought he was doing something spectacular and secretive, I already knew about it. So when Rod called me to ask where to bill the retainer for whatever Princeton was doing with that girl, since it wasn't business related, I told him exactly what any father in my situation would tell him; avoid the meeting and cancel the retainer. PJ had no children so why he was going above and beyond for this girl and her baby, when he had a list of other things to do had me confused. He should've just bought her a happy meal and a bottle of formula and kept it moving. Since he seemed so stuck on this girl however, I knew that I had to do something to keep this girl from attaching herself to my son like a hungry leech. Then knowing exactly what time their appointment was scheduled for, I dressed my best and headed to Rod's office. Whether Princeton liked it or not, they both were about to learn how much I disapproved of this relationship. I quickly alerted my driver that it was time to go and I beat Princeton there by a good fifteen minutes, waiting in my car until I saw him, that girl and that bastard child walk into his office. Then I got out and made my way in.

Princeton didn't see me until the knocking noise that my cane made became closer and closer. But when we made eye contact, Princeton wore that same scared look he wore as a child whenever his mother and I caught him doing something he had no business doing.

"Dad, what are you doing here?" he asked, looking like a deer caught in the headlights. "I didn't know that you had any meetings with Rod today." He stammered and I had to keep myself from laughing in his face and embarrassing my son in front of his little friend.

"I don't. But I know that you do and I had to come here to keep you from making yourself look stupid, Princeton." I lectured, turning to Peyton to make sure that she heard me loud and clear. "Young lady, I don't know what illusion my son has you under, but my family can't be of any more assistance to you. Prince & Parrish is not a non-profit organization. We work for funds, not for fun." Snarling, I watched tears creep up to her eyes, but she worked hard to keep them from falling and blinked them away. I usually hated to be the bad guy, especially having to break the heart of pretty young thing like Peyton, but if that's what I had to do to keep my empire and my legacy together, then so be it. Princeton didn't understand but one day, when he became a father, he would.

Princeton looked between me and her, his entire face becoming red in embarrassment but if he was expecting me to apologize for my words, he had another thing coming.

"I shouldn't have come here..." she muttered under her breath, as I couldn't help the smile that creeped over my face as I held my victory.

"It's always best if you follow your first mind. Don't worry. You're still young, you'll learn." If my parents had taught me one thing, it was how to get under a bitch's skin. To make her doubt everything she thought she knew was a gift, but I'd had it for years. Grabbing her bag, she pulled away from Princeton when he grabbed her by the wrist. "Don't. Touch. Me," she seethed. "Don't you dare put your hands on me." Pulling her jacket back to her, she readjusted her daughter on her hip and then walked off, ignoring the curious stares of everyone around us. Princeton followed behind her for a short time, calling her name like a little, sick puppy until she was too far for him to catch up to. Turning back in my direction, Princeton was on fire as he stormed my way. I knew he was coming straight for me, so I wiped the smile off my face and put my business façade back on.

"What the fuck was that, dad? What are you trying to do, ruin my life?" he asked, as I shook my head. I attempted to put my hand on his shoulder, but it was still too soon for that and he shrugged it off.

"Princeton James Parrish... You don't understand right now, but one day, when you have a child, you will understand. I can't let you ruin your life with someone who has nothing going in theirs. She is a high school *drop-out*, son... and she has a child already. You have your Master's degree. You two are not the same. Didn't I always teach you to not play house? If you aren't going to have a child with someone who isn't your wife, why would you play daddy to a child who isn't yours with someone who isn't your wife?" I asked, trying to get him to look at it a different way. People in the lawyer's office were staring at me judgmentally, but I didn't care. Until they held a position that I held, it wasn't like they would understand. Unlike the average person, we actually had shit to lose when it came to scandals like this. We had everything to lose.

Princeton was similar to his mother in a lot of ways and his stubbornness was one of them, but unlike his mother, I was unfazed by my son's antics.

"Stay the fuck out of my life. I can't help it that you're a coldhearted nigga whose never loved anybody besides himself." Princeton insulted me, like that was supposed to hurt my feelings.

"I'm just trying to keep you from making the biggest mistake of your life." I shouted after him, as he walked away from me. When he flipped me the bird, I laughed. No matter what he said, my job was done. Sort of. Knowing that I needed to polish off one final end, I pulled my phone out and placed a call. Knowing she'd answer, I smiled when on the second ring, she picked up. "Della, my sweet thing. Mi amor.... I think you need to come in to town. We need to talk."

Chapter Nine

"THE FEELINGS YOU DESIRE,"

PEYTON TAHJ EVER.

I wasn't thinking when I left Princeton behind obviously, because I knew that eventually, we had to get back in the same exact car. I wasn't about to call myself being mad, walk down the streets of the Chicago to the bus stop and get shot dead with my baby, all because I was too proud to get in the car. I could see his arms flailing and he was clearly raising his voice as he talked to his dad but I had no idea what he was saying. Our driver was a female and after hearing me sniffle as I attempted to dry up my tears, she rolled down the partition and handed me a box of Kleenex.

"Thank you, Miss." I accepted, putting Taylen back in her car-seat as I blew my nose and attempted not to start sobbing again.

"Never stop fighting." The woman said, after I had visibly calmed down. My face wasn't red any more and I could feel my breathing becoming controlled again so I relaxed. I wanted to ask the woman what she meant but apparently my face said it all because she looked in the rearview mirror and started to chuckle under her breath. "If that is the person you love, then never stop fighting... Pause for a moment if you have to, but never stop fighting for him. Sometimes it's hard for them to see what they have. Men aren't as smart as us." She actually managed to get a smile from me. After a few moments, Princeton entered the car and I made one thing very clear.

"You don't have to speak to me. Don't look at me. Don't even think my way until we get to the hotel. I need some time to cool off and don't want to say something I might regret." I spoke finally, putting my mommy voice on. Surprisingly, he didn't even argue. He just sat back and enjoyed the ride. When we got to the hotel suite, Princeton immediately went into the back and began placing phone calls. I was trying to ignore him, because I was still mad, but it was hard to not hear that he was talking about me. The entire ride, I couldn't help but think that maybe if I was in Princeton's position, I would do the same thing. After all, it wasn't like my family were multi-millionaires so I had never been in that situation. Putting Taylen down because she was past due for a nap, I walked into the same room as him and stood there. I wasn't trying to be nosey or anything, but if it involved my daughter and I, then I deserved to know.

"Hi Antonio. This is Princeton Parrish, I received your number from Nino. Would you have time for a consultation this afternoon or evening? I really need to have a very important matter resolved and I know you're the perfect person for the job. I can send over retainer immediately." Knowing he wouldn't ask any questions when he saw how much money Princeton was talking, I watched as he quickly got his routing information and personally made sure that $300,000 showed up in the lawyer's account. I was grateful and impressed, because there were no limits to what he would do for my daughter and I. I don't care what anyone said, that was sexy as hell. He watched, while he remained on the phone, the money appear in his account and I could tell that he was getting nervous.

"Are you in town now, Mr. Parrish?"

"Yes, I am. Could we meet in like an hour?"

"An hour sounds good. See you then." When Princeton turned to me after the lawyer had hung up, all of the madness I felt quickly vanished. He was the only man who ever had that effect on me.

"I keep telling you I'm not that man, Peyton. My

dad thinks he's smart, but I'm smarter. If you ride with me a little longer, I promise you that I can show you you're safe. You're used to running but you don't have to do that with me. Whenever you're ready to go, we can go get something to eat and then go meet with the lawyer about acquiring whatever we need to acquire to keep Taylen here with us. Alright?" I was speechless so I just nodded my head. I wanted to jump on him, but I knew that with us having somewhere to be, that probably wasn't a good idea. I quickly got Taylen awake and ready to head out again, even ignoring her spoiled self screaming at the top of her lungs because I knew that as soon as we got back into the car, she would fall right back to sleep.

The drive was relatively quick and after Ig a bite to eat from the drive-thru, we were on our way to the attorney's office. My nerves were getting the best of me, and the moment that I pulled a chicken sandwich out of the bag, I lost my appetite. All I could think about was losing my baby. This was causing my mind to play tricks on me and had me strongly doubting my ability to be a good mom. *Maybe Taylen would be better off with Shondell.* As quickly as the thought entered my head, I shook it off physically. After forty-two and a half hours of active labor with my baby girl,

I knew for a fact that there was nobody in the world who could love her more than me. I would never give anyone else the satisfaction of raising her or being able to claim Taylen Ella Tahj Ever as theirs. She was mine, through and through. As if he could sense my doubt, Princeton leaned over and grabbed my hand in his, kissing my palm gently. "Just watch. This lawyer is going to give us some good news. I can feel it." Princeton smiled at me and surprisingly, I believed him.

Something had me feeling like Princeton was my good luck charm. Besides the fact that all the black women in the woman were staring at me jealously for being the one by Princeton's side, the lawyer seemed in a rush to give us good news. After some digging, they'd found old warrants for Shondell. Since they were from so long ago, they were void but it didn't matter. It still helped with our case, because all we had to do was show that Shondell's home was an unstable environment for my baby. I had complete faith that we could do that. Besides, Princeton had recorded Shondell threatening me and calling me out of my name the entire time we talked on the phone. It was a relief to hear that the lawyer believed we had enough evidence to prove that Taylen shouldn't be placed with her grandma. After he had delivered the good news, the lawyer leaned forward and folded his hands together.

"Have you thought about adoption, Ms. Ever?" he asked politely. For some reason, I took what he was saying the wrong way and Princeton must have been able to tell because he quickly grabbed my hand in an attempt to relax me. At that point, the lawyer must have realized that I misconstrued his words because he immediately began to edit what he had said. "You're misunderstanding me. Have you ever thought about allowing Princeton to adopt Taylen?" he clarified.

I wasn't sure what to say but it was making me nervous that Princeton was really just staring at me and not saying anything. I knew that Taylen being my baby made it my decision alone, but to be put on the spot like that was completely unfair to me.

"I- I need some time to think about that," I stuttered, shifting in my seat. I had no other option but to sit there and pray that the subject of adoption would change to something else. Anything else, actually.

With my baby's dad not being alive, yes I knew that I needed to move on for the sake of me and my baby, but that didn't mean that I wanted to erase him completely from Taylen's life. To put so much pressure on me about something that was as important and life-changing as adopting my daughter seemed wrong to me, but he wasn't grasping that. Luckily, Princeton had enough sense to tell that I was uncomfortable and quickly moved on with the conversation. I blocked most of it out because it was useless to me. We had gotten exactly what we came for and now, we needed to leave. Luckily for me, it seemed that Taylen was on my team and began to cry loudly, letting Princeton know that it was time to go. I'm sure that during the drive, Princeton could tell something was wrong. I didn't even bother hiding that I was in my feelings. He drove in silence, the only sound between us being the tapping of his fingers on the steering wheel. Usually, I would have let him start up the conversation but not this time. "No matter what you think, Princeton... Taylen will always need her dad. Talon will always be a part of her. I refuse to take that away from her, just because you want to be the one she calls daddy. I appreciate everything you've done for us, don't get me wrong... But trying to remove a part of her is wrong." I know that my words hurt Princeton's feelings because I basically watched the air leave his lungs and maybe I didn't word my thoughts correctly, but by the time they came out of my mouth, it was already too late.

"That's what you think? I'm trying to take Taylen away from her father?" Princeton asked, and I began to look straightforward. If I had made this whole big thing out of nothing, I was about to be super embarrassed.

"Princeton, I-," I knew that I'd made a really bad decision and I was trying to mend the mess that I was about to get myself into. I could tell by Princeton's face though, that I was just about to dig myself into a bigger hole. He wasn't hearing anything I had to say.

"All I've ever done is show you why you should be with me! I just transferred $300,000 to this lawyer so that you can keep your daughter and now I'm trying to take her away from her father? Her dad is dead, Peyton! He's gone and you sulking over that isn't going to change the fact that with or without me, Taylen is going to have to grow up without him." By this point, he was yelling. I understood his frustration and he was right, so I dropped my head and shut up as he went on and on. Eventually, he stopped talking. I don't know if he figured I wasn't listening or what, but he turned the music back up while I stared out of the window. After a long while of driving, I gathered that we weren't going back to the hotel but I was too scared to ask Princeton our destination. I knew that a massive, explosive argument was just over the horizons and if I didn't approach carefully, our estimated arrival time would be sooner rather than later. Eventually, I watched as he pulled into Parrish & Prince's driveway and I immediately began to clutch my seatbelt. If Princeton thought I was about to go in there and face his father, he had another thing coming. After everything Kingston had said, he never had to worry about me again.

Unfortunately, Princeton wouldn't allow me to ignore the fact that he was sitting next to me with his hand out, refusing to accept any other answer but yes. "I'm sorry for not sticking up for you with my father. But if you allow me to, I'm about to handle all of that." My mind was screaming for me to say hell no and run the opposite way but with Princeton being so forceful and unwilling to hear the word no, it was hard to. So sucking it up and putting my big girl panties on, I took a few deep breaths and then got out of the car. By that time, he had put Taylen in the stroller and locked the car up. When he grabbed me by the hand and led us into the building, I felt like the most important woman in the world.

Princeton's father was definitely surprised to see

us, but so were the other ten people that Kingston Sr. was apparently having a meeting with. I immediately attempted to turn around and make a run for it, but he held my hand tightly, holding me in place. Kingston seemed perturbed but played it calm as he completely ignored us as if I didn't have a babbling baby talking her lungs out in the middle of the conference room. Princeton stood still and didn't move a muscle, but he also didn't back down. He stood up straight and maintained eye contact with his father. I felt like I was in the middle of a brawl between Scar and Mufasa. It didn't matter who claimed the victory at the end, because it seemed like either way, I was going to be the one that ended up getting mauled. After all, there was no way that I would come between father and son. At least, that's what I thought.

"Princeton, there are no extras allowed in here during conference times. You know that."

"Peyton isn't an extra. You know that, so don't play with me dad. She's my future wife and as of yesterday, she's my business partner." This got his attention just as quickly as it got mine, and we both ended up looking at Princeton at the same time.

"Huh?" I asked. He squeezed my hand to signal me to shut up, but if he thought that was going to work, he was absolutely right. I wanted to see how this was going to play out. I was actually wishing that I had a camera so I could film Kingston's face, but I did my best to hold my laughter in.

"Excuse me?" Kingston asked, finally looking away from his presentation long enough to make eye contact with Princeton. "Any business partner of yours is a business partner of mine. You can't do that without consulting me first." He snapped, and I watched in hysteria as Princeton's smile took over his face.

"Actually, I can. As of yesterday, you are no longer Parrish & Prince, Inc. You're just Parrish, Inc. I've branched out on my own." Pulling some papers out of his briefcase, I watched in amazement as he presented them to his dad and watched as he read them. Everyone around the two was starting to feel the same as me; that they were caught into a massive brawl and we were all about to be innocent bystanders.

"Can everyone please give us a moment?" Kingston asked politely, even though I could tell that he wanted to flash. The people sitting in chairs quickly heeded his warning and bounced. I attempted to give them some time for their conversation but Princeton was once again holding me in place.

"Nah, you stay." He ordered, not even taking his eyes off of his father.

"So that's what you're going to do? You picked her over your own family? Your own fortune?" Kingston snarled, the disgust written all over his face. "Over what? Over *her?* What can she do for you? Son, you can find better pussy. Shit, I can buy you some." That's when Princeton drew the line and stepping forward, I was sure that they were about to fight so I pulled him back to me.

"Prince, it's okay. I promise. It didn't hurt my feelings." I was trying to calm Princeton down, but it seemed to only make things worse. Kingston turned to me and smirked. He opened his mouth to say something, but Princeton cut him off. He probably already knew his father's words were about to be rude and belligerent.

"No, it's not okay." Princeton turned to me and did something I would have never expected. He kissed me right in front of his dad, and I'm not speaking about one of our other kisses. Princeton kissed me until my knees began to shiver and when I pulled away from him, Kingston was still standing there and watching us like a lion hungry for prey. "Dad, Peyton makes me feel something I've never felt with you. She makes me happy. She doesn't love me because of what I do for her, I do for her because I love her... which is something you wouldn't understand because you only do for others when there's something in it for you. My lawyer, who's not Rod, will be in touch with the proper paperwork later this week." With that, Princeton grabbed my hand as we pushed the stroller away and headed back to the car. I felt so bad that all of this was really because of me, but it really showed me who Princeton was.

"Maybe I should just go back to Boston. All of this will be a lot easier. I feel responsible for you and your dad falling out, Princeton." I whispered as we got into the elevator to take us to the parking garage. He pulled me into his chest and I instantly relaxed as I felt the smell of his cologne seep its way into my nose and into my bloodstream.

"No, no more running Peyton. Whatever issues we have, we'll face them together. Alright?" he asked, kissing the top of my head as I nodded. I was trying to keep my thug composure together but I still allowed a few tears to slip out. When we got to the car, he loaded Taylen in and we headed out. Stuck at a stoplight, Princeton must have decided to just unleash everything on me at once. "I think you should move in with me, when we get back to Cleveland." He suggested and my eyes bulged out of my head.

"So you're just going to move your ex bitch out and move another one in, huh?" I halfway joked, before Princeton mushed my face.

"Jersey has never been to my Cleveland house, so don't get confused, Peyton. I'd never eat you out on the same sheets another woman has laid on. I value you too much." Grabbing his hand, I couldn't have hidden the smile all over my face if I wanted to. Unfortunately, it didn't last that long. When we pulled into the valet parking and got out, it was clear that we weren't alone and I recognized the voice that I heard yelling. It was Princeton's ex. Turning to him, he obviously read my thoughts because he grabbed my hands, probably not wanting me to lay the poor girl out again.

"Princeton, I'm telling you this because I do not want to be a bad look for you…" I seethed, through clenched teeth. "You better handle her or I will."

Chapter Ten

"SAVE ME BEING HONEST, BABY."

JERSEY JAE JUDD.

Checking my phone as I waited for Kingston's text back, I felt the strongest sense of anger I'd ever felt after reading the message he sent me. It was crazy how things worked out, because I was back in Chicago visiting family and checking in with my son. But after what Princeton's dad told me, all of that would have to wait for a moment because I needed some answers and only Princeton could give them to me.

Let's make this clear, because I know you all don't know me very well. I had never been the "bust your windows out" type of girl, but when you have had as much time with P.J as I have, you understand. It's not easy to just throw all of that away, just because he was 'trying' to move on. After getting so close to becoming Mrs. Princeton James Parrish, there was no way that I was about to let some nobody with a baby get in the way of PJ and I. Not when I had a baby of my own to think about. Okay, well... full disclosure. My "baby" wasn't really a baby any more. Jaxxon James Judd, my pride and joy, was almost six years old and still had yet to meet his father, but I was in no rush to deal with the drama that I knew would stem from that. At least... I hadn't been in a rush until the man I hoped I would one day call my father in law, texted me to tell me that the love of my life was intent, and determined, to marry someone else, who hadn't put nearly the same amount of time and dedication into Princeton that I had. That just wouldn't happen, at least not on my watch. So now, here I was. Standing in front of the hotel lobby where Peyton and Princeton were staying, like some sort of protester. I was just waiting to see a glimpse of PJ's face when he saw me, or when his "girlfriend" realized that I would need more than a brutal beating to keep me from getting my man back. Kingston was on his way to the hotel when we spoke and I could tell that something had transpired between the two of them, just by the way that Kingston was talking. I wasn't sure what it was, but it couldn't have been good.

I spotted Peyton and Princeton walking into the hotel lobby but I got to them before they even caught a glimpse of me. He was pushing the stroller with Peyton's baby inside and the visual image instantly made me madder than I already was. Knowing there was no way that I would get close to Peyton, or PJ for that matter without getting hit again, I did the only thing I could think of to do. I took my shoe off, aimed in their direction, and then watched it fly into the air like a white dove. I was trying to hit Princeton in his head but I gasped when the shoe instead flew into the stroller and hit Peyton's baby, causing her to start screaming at the top of her lungs. I would've apologized but I knew that even speaking to Peyton would cause me to get beat up, and I didn't want that issue. When I looked up, Peyton was being held back by Princeton. Something told me that was my signal to go, but my feet were frozen to the floor. Soon, and obviously without my subconscious telling me not to be stupid, I approached them. I knew the best thing to do was simply walk away, but the anger that raged through my bloodstream wouldn't allow it.

"Does she know that you killed our baby? Huh?" I spewed, watching as Peyton's eyes nearly bulged out of her head. Though it wasn't the exact truth, I knew what to say to get under a woman's skin. Especially a mother. Princeton stood there cluelessly, probably trying to figure out what to tell his female while Peyton waited for an answer. Meanwhile, I knew I wasn't helping the situation but that was the most fun part about it. "I bet he didn't tell you that, huh? He's over here playing house with your baby, but made me get rid of ours! What about your own baby, Princeton? Your flesh and blood?" PJ was frustrated and I watched contently, muffling a laugh as I literally watched their relationship crumble. I couldn't even lie and say I wasn't enjoying it, because it was written all over my face.

"That was high school, Jersey! We were kids! What do you want me to say about it? We weren't ready to be parents." He screamed, now getting the attention of everyone else around us. I felt like a spectacle in a museum and before I could control it, my hand had struck across his cheek like a lightning bolt. Princeton wasn't particularly dark or light, but either way, my hand definitely left a visible imprint on his face. His little Chihuahua stepped forward, but I put my hand in front of me, signaling her to back up.

"Don't come near me. I will call the police on you." I warned Peyton and she lifted her hands up in surrender. However, she did make sure that I understood clearly her next warning.

"Listen. I'm going to warn you once... and once only. You and Princeton's issues belong to you two, and you two only... That has nothing to do with me, so I have no issue with you over him or with the fact that you were with him before I was. What I have an issue with is the disrespect. Popping up at my home, and the hotel we're staying in. Those are all petty things to do, but not disrespectful. With that being said, I start to take things really personally when it comes to Taylen. So the next time you intentionally, or unintentionally involve my daughter in your mess, I will forget that I'm an educated young woman with a whole lot to lose and I will beat your ass." She snapped, grabbing the stroller from PJ and walking into the lobby.

"Is this really what you're about now, Jersey? This shit is getting to be too much. You're really looking like a psycho out here. You need some help." Princeton told me, and I instantly felt my heart drop. My lips began to quiver and I could feel the tears threatening to roll down my cheeks but I refused to give him the joy of seeing that he'd broken me for the last time. I knew that it was time for me to go, so I prepared to walk off but then Princeton walked so close to me that I thought he was about to hit me. Just out of instinct, I flinched. He brought his hand as close to me as he could while I tried my hardest not to wince, but my breath was caught in my throat as I thought about what could happen next. "I'm going to tell you this one time only. Stay the hell away from me, Peyton and Taylen." With that being said, he turned and walked into the hotel lobby like a sad puppy looking for his master.

I heard a loud honk behind me and when I turned around to look, I couldn't help but smile. Princeton was constantly dogging me out, but where his son lacked, Kingston made up for it. Therefore, whatever he wanted me to do, whenever, I was down for it. Skipping to the limo, I opened the door and slid in, pulling my skirt down so it reached my knees again. Kingston sat there with a smile on his face but I was surprised to see an older woman sitting beside him with a grim smirk on her face. Her presence kind of scared me, to be honest.

"Oh, I didn't realize we had company." I murmured, watching as the woman began to laugh.

"Listen, sweetie... I'm not here to interrupt whatever it is that you have going on with Kingy... I'm just here to help you, help me." After that, I was pulled out of the limo and that's all I remember.

THE LOVE WE HAD

Chapter Eleven

"TAKE IT HOW YOU WANT IT."

PRINCETON JAMES PARRISH.

Peyton and I made our way into the hotel lobby and then to our room, where we both sprawled out on the bed, too exhausted to even speak on the situation with Jersey. Instead though, I curled up next to Peyton and put my head in the soft spot between her neck and shoulder, inhaling her sweet smell. My face was so close to her skin that I could practically taste her perfume. My breath must have tickled her because she pushed me away, laughing hysterically. Then I laid my head in her lap while I turned the TV on and scrolled through, looking for something to watch. Thought I'd never admit it to Peyton, at least not right now, all I could think about was putting a ring on her finger and making it official as we worked on expanding our family.

Eventually, I felt Peyton's breathing slow down and I knew that she was asleep without even looking at her. I rubbed her stomach, knowing that soon enough, my heir would be in progress. I could feel it. Eventually, my mind started to wander off as I thought about Jersey's pregnancy and remembering everything that happened back then. Every single day since I took her to the clinic, I thought about that baby. My son, or daughter, would have been almost eight years old. I couldn't help but wonder what they would look like, or how they would act. Would he or she be calm and collected like me or loud and belligerent like Jersey?

Sighing, I buried my head further into Peyton's lap as I prayed for those thoughts to leave my mind. I didn't need any additional stress, especially about a situation so long ago that I had no control over now. That was as far as my thoughts went before I passed out, joining Peyton in a deep sleep.

It seemed like we slept for hours but my eyes fluttered open and the first thing that I noticed was that someone was banging on our door. Taylen was screaming and Peyton hopped up. We both exchanged confused glances and I got up to see who it was. Before I could even get to the door though, it was kicked in and police swarmed in with their guns drawn. Peyton was screaming as she tried to make it to Taylen, who was still in the stroller. Unfortunately, there was so many of them and not enough of us. They quickly buried my face in the floor while I tried to calm Peyton down, but we were both freaking out. I'd never been in trouble in my life and didn't know what this was about, but the cops weren't saying anything, no matter how much I asked. Clasping handcuffs around my wrist, they lifted me up by my arms and dragged me out.

That was almost six weeks ago and I was still sitting in jail. All my calls to Peyton went unanswered and I was worried as fuck that something had happened to her while they were pinning me up in here. Everything that they were charging me with was bogus, but it was okay. I had my lawyers on it and I knew that I would be getting out sooner rather than later. There was no way that people were about to keep me in here for something I didn't do. I had a business to get off the ground.

My hair was starting to get scruffy and used to going to the barbershop once every two weeks to keep my appearance up to par, I was going crazy in here. So when I heard that I had a visitor, my heart skipped a beat. Maybe Peyton had gotten my messages after all of this time, but that didn't stop me from being angry with her, especially after worrying for nearly a month. I didn't know if something had happened to her or Taylen and the thought of that scared the hell out of me.

But when they lead me to the visiting room and I saw who was waiting for me, that anger came back and my excitement vanished. That was the last person I wanted to see. I thought about turning around and telling the guards I wasn't interested, but after being alone with my cellmate for way too long, I would happily accept a meeting from a familiar face, even if I hated his guts right now.

"Hello, PJ." My dad said, smiling as he sat down. I could tell that he was getting enjoyment out of this, but I remained quiet. After our last exchange I knew that something was up, I was just waiting for it. When he produced a white envelope and opened it, I tapped my foot on the ground as he slid it over to me. I knew by the handwriting that it was Peyton's and just by how long it was, I knew exactly what it was. It hurt, especially after all I'd done for Peyton and her baby but I wouldn't let my father know that. Especially while he was standing across from me with that stupid smile on his face.

"You're enjoying this, aren't you?" I muttered, even

though I already knew the answer. Everything in my dad's body language gave me the answer.

"Well I do like when my children learn the lesson I was trying to teach the entire time. I told you that girl meant you no good, Princeton. I've said that from the beginning. She just wanted you for what you could do for her, not how you make her feel. You should've left her alone a long-," I couldn't control my anger anymore and hit the table. When I popped up, the guards immediately came over and gave me a warning to sit down and calm down.

"Damn it, dad! You think that's what I need to hear while I'm in here? A lecture? I didn't even do anything!" I yelled as loud as I could without getting toted back to my cell. I hadn't even looked at the letter but the shit sitting in front of me left a sinking feeling in my stomach, so I quickly hid it in my pocket and waited for the guard to guide me back to my cell.

The moment I got into my cell, I knocked over everything I could find as I went into the biggest meltdown I'd ever had. Peyton really played me. She got what she wanted and she bounced. That had to be the worst thing I'd ever felt. That's when I decided to sit down and read what Peyton wrote me, as if it made a difference.

Dear Princeton,

I don't know the spot I'm supposed to have in your life. It seems that fate is always playing around and bringing us back together, but I'm not sure that's even the way it's supposed to be. It seems that I bring nothing but trouble and drams to your life and for that, I am truly sorry. We have nothing in common, Princeton. Your life and my life are completely different and I'm not sure our worlds will ever be able to merge peacefully. You deserve a woman, not a bitch with a baby. I love you, Princeton. I always have and I always will. That is why I'm doing this. Just watch. In the end, you'll see that this is what's best.

Peyton

I knew this was Peyton's handwriting, so she had definitely been the one to write this but something just didn't seem right to me. I needed to get the hell out of here so I could figure out exactly what was going on with her.

Chapter Twelve

"DO YOU LOVE ME FOR A MOMENT?"

PEYTON TAHJ EVER.

Five and a half weeks prior...

Watching them drag Princeton out of the hotel room like a common criminal, I can't even lie. My brain froze, but I managed to grab Taylen and follow out behind them while they took him out to the car.

"What are you doing? He didn't do anything!" I yelled louder than I meant to, scaring Taylen who began to cry. I rocked her to calm her down, but it didn't matter. To the officers, I must've looked like Casper because they looked right through me as they continued to put my baby in the back of the car. When they drove away, I stood there, flabbergasted. Things had escalated and now I wasn't sure what to do, but I knew that someone needed to help him because I had no idea where to start. Something told me that this was all my fault and I refused to let him sit and rot because he'd done so much for me.

Honestly, I didn't want to admit but day after day, I was starting to fall more in love with Princeton.

Calling to my job, I quickly got a hold of Corie, my boss. She'd helped me so many times and in so many different ways. I knew that she could help me this time, or at least give me the knowledge of what to do. Apparently, she didn't hear something off in my voice because the moment that I got patched through to her direct line, she began to ramble.

"Are you enjoying your vacation?" she asked and I couldn't help myself. I instantly started crying. "What is it? What's wrong, honey?"

"Listen, I need your help. I didn't know who else to call." I said after I finally managed to calm myself down. After explaining everything to her and not hearing a response, I waited for an answer. "Corie, are you there?" I asked, checking the screen to make sure our call hadn't disconnected.

"Yes, I'm here. Peyton, this is truly a hard subject. Either way, it's a sensitive subject. Whether or not Princeton is innocent, bad publicity like this could be devastating for us. Especially as a new company... If you do decide to stay there and support him, I'll have no choice but terminate your employment here with us. I'm sorry..." With that, she hung up and a knot began to form in my throat. Not having a job to come back to wasn't a big deal, because I knew that it would be easy for me to get another one, but income security was a big problem for me and I'd just gotten to the point where I began to save enough for a rainy day. It was bittersweet, but I knew I could handle it. I'd made it with way less before. The only downfall was that without Corie, I literally had nobody to help me get Princeton out. The more I thought about it though, I knew there was one person who would bail Princeton out, even it was on his own conditions, I literally had no other option. Unlocking Prince's phone, I pulled up his dad's number and dialed it.

He played it cool, but I knew Kingston was surprised to hear from me. I could hear it in his voice. I wanted to keep our conversation short and straight to the point, so I quickly explained what happened but I noticed his voice didn't change the entire time that we talked. I wanted to show him that I'd truly surrendered and that he won, so I lowered my voice as I prepared to plead.

"Mr. Parrish... I know you hate me. I'll be out of your way, just please help Princeton. He doesn't deserve this... I'll do whatever you want me to do." I hoped and prayed that he didn't take what I said the wrong way. There was no way that I was going *that* far. My love had limits. Before I knew it, he was sending me an address and telling me to meet him in an hour before hanging up in my face. Just in case I needed to leave right after, I packed bags for me and Taylen, along with everything else I would need. I then securely tucked my pepper spray in my pocket just in case Princeton's dad got bold. By the time I got Taylen changed and ready, it was time for us to head out. I didn't want to make Kingston mad by having him wait, though a little dose of patience was exactly what he needed.

I made it to the diner and quickly grabbed Taylen up, even though we were right on time. We went inside and I quickly got us seated. Only a few minutes later, Kingston was sitting down to join Taylen and I. When a waitress came over to our table, he looked over at me.

"You can order whatever you want. I'll pay." I internally rolled my eyes because he was a crazy, pompous bastard if he thought I couldn't pay for my own food. I looked over the menu as fast as I could, and ordered something that I knew wouldn't take that long to prepare. I didn't want to have to be around him any longer than necessary. Kingston, on the other hand, ordered over-easy eggs, toast, potato hash and a deck of chocolate chip pancakes. After the waitress was gone, Kingston turned back to me. "I need you to write a letter. Something that sounds like you, about why you can't be with my son." After saying that, he slid a black bag in my direction. I almost unzipped it, but he stopped me. "Don't open that in here." He whispered, looking out of the window as talked, avoiding any sort of eye contact with me. He hadn't looked me in my eyes since he got here. Kingston was the most intimidating man I'd ever met in my life and he didn't have to say anything. My heart was about to somersault through my throat and I was trying to avoid throwing up out of nervousness. "In there is $200,000. Consider it an incentive to stay away." He thought he was getting over on me, but I wasn't worried about the money. I immediately thought about cursing him out, but I still needed him to help Princeton so I closed my mouth and kept my thoughts to myself. "As far as my conditions... you are not to return home. I know my son and he'll follow you to the ends of the earth, trying to figure out what happened. You're going to change your number and you're never going to talk to Princeton again. In the meantime, it will be like this never happened. Like you and Princeton never happened." I almost cried when he said that, but I knew the truth so I kept calm.

The fire that Princeton ignited in my mind, body and soul was a fire that was hard to extinguish. It could've rained for forty days and nights and I would still feel that heat between us. No amount of money could make me forget the special connection that we shared, even in the short time that we were together. When Kingston was sure that I understood him clearly, he handed me a piece of notebook paper and a pen. "Good. Now write the letter." Ignoring the tears as I wrote, I poured my heart out onto that paper, since that was the last time I'd get a chance to tell him how I felt. After I finished, I left a kiss on the bottom of the paper. Then I handed it back over to Kingston. Soon after, the waitress came back and delivered our food to the table. I quickly ate and cooled some oatmeal off so I could give it to Taylen, while I waited for him to finish.

"I'm going to do what I said I'll do... I'll stay away. But you're not going to go back on your word, are you? How do I know I can trust you?" It seemed like a justifiable question to me, but he seemed offended by it. Regardless, I waited for an answer. I wasn't leaving until he looked me in my eyes and promised that he would get

Princeton out. Nothing else was worrying me, at this point. When he smiled at me, I instantly discovered where Princeton got his charm from. If Kingston wasn't so manipulative, it would be easy to see how cunning he was.

"Trust me, Peyton... There's a lot more for me to gain from PJ being out here than there is from him being locked up in there." He finished his food and then slapped a hundred-dollar bill on the table. "I'll take you to the airport." The way he talked, I could tell that he was ordering me around, but in a nice way. I didn't bother arguing with him, I just picked my daughter up, grabbed the black bag and followed behind him quietly. By the time we made it out to his car, someone already was loading my bags into his trunk.

I remained quiet the whole ride, a victim of my own thoughts and it seemed that Princeton's dad was still in the same boat. I watched him pass a glance at me and Taylen every now and then, but other than that, the ride was completely silent between us two. Just how I liked it. When we finally pulled in front of the airport, Kingston got out to keep the door open for me so I could get Taylen and my bags out. I paid special attention to making sure that the black bag Kingston had given me was tucked

THE LOVE WE HAD

away neatly and out of sight. My daughter and I walked into the airport and I could feel his eyes on me the whole time, burning a hole into the back of my head. I know that he thought I would go back on my word, but as long as he made sure Prince was taken care of, nobody would ever have to worry about me again. Looking at the gigantic map, I realized I'd come here with no specific destination in mind. Taylen was into pointing now, so I decided to ask her.

"Alright, baby doll... it's your turn to choose. Where to, next?" She quickly leaned into the map and when I was sure that she was pointing to one particular area, I smiled. "That's my baby..."

Present Day...

Waking up to see that Taylen was still sprawled out on my mattress, I crept into the bathroom. After washing my face and brushing my teeth, I went to make some breakfast before my baby woke up. She'd gotten a stomach bug the week before from some little grubby kids at daycare, and was just now starting to feel better. Unfortunately, sleeping in the bed next to me had its pros and cons and now, I was starting to feel a little under the weather. Still, it was a workday which meant that it was time to get

Taylen ready to go, so that I could get to work. Just like I suspected, getting a job was no problem. Four days after landing in Phoenix, Arizona, I landed a job with the Make-A-Wish foundation, as a public relations leader for brand communication. To make a long story short, I dealt with the high-profile investors, the celebrities who liked to remain anonymous in order to make their donations in peace, while still being able to see where their money is going to. My days were long and hard, but the pay was pretty good and I was easily able to keep a roof over Taylen and I's head. I still thought of Princeton every day, but I used the hotel's WiFi to check jails in Chicago. As promised, he was freed from jail.

Glancing from the window to my baby girl, I sighed sadly. She was starting to get so big so quickly and was just now starting to scoot and be able to eat solids. I'd gotten the green light from her doctor to start giving her a small amount of eggs at a time so I scrambled one, put half on the plate for her to eat and then the other half on my breakfast bagel. After only about two or three bites, I was over it. The eggs didn't taste right and it left a bad taste in my mouth, so after gagging, I threw it out and went to get a cup of orange juice.

I knew it was because I was coming down with something, so I shook off the thought of having something else to eat before work. I didn't want to be nauseous during the day so I just prepared myself to go in. Once I finished getting Taylen ready, we headed out and I hurriedly dropped her off at daycare before going my own way. The moment that I stepped into the building at work, I got a sinking feeling in my stomach, and I knew better than to doubt my instinct. The last time I felt like this, Taylen's father died. *Something was off.* My feelings changed when I walked into the office with my name on it and watched the view from inside the sixth story window. At only eighteen, I had something that a lot of people didn't have. There were a lot of thirty-year olds that I knew that didn't have my position, let alone some of the people the same age as me. Regardless, I couldn't have been more grateful, especially after knowing how far I'd come. When my work phone rang and jolted me out of my thoughts, I got to my chair and pretended like I was actually doing some work. I assumed it was my boss checking in for the day, so my white girl voice was in full effect, except it wasn't my boss at all. As a matter of fact, it wasn't a voice I'd ever heard before.

"Ms. Ever... Hello, how are you doing today?" the man sounded like he was in his 40's and he was definitely black. He was starting to make me nervous, but I kept it calm while I waited for him to continue speaking. It was clear that he was waiting for something else though.

"I'm sorry... It seems like you know me, but I don't know you. Who is this?" I asked politely, not wanting to come off as rude. My heart was starting to beat through my chest and my anxiety was through the roof.

"This is Detective Phoenix with Cleveland's homicide division..." I was confused as hell until I heard a name slip from his mouth. My heart then stopped and it was a good thing I was already sitting down because I felt like the muscles in my legs became like limp, overcooked spaghetti noodles. The phone fell from my hands and a scream escaped my lips before my brain could even process that I was still at work/ I heard people coming into my office, but at that moment in time, everything but the detective's words was a blur, a broken record stuck in slow motion.

I could feel my panic attack sneaking up on me so I hurriedly put my knees to my chest and began rocking back and forth. I'm sure I looked like a mental patient, but I wasn't worried about it. I didn't even manage to calm myself down until I heard my boss's voice. It was at that moment I attempted to get myself together but as I stood up, my vision still blurry and my heart still racing, I just knew that I was about to be fired. Instead I looked up to see her shooing everyone out of the room, demanding that they give me some space and privacy. That's when I remembered Detective Phoenix was still on the line and I rushed to pick the phone back up. "I understand how difficult this is for you, Ms. Ever and I'm sorry to have to ask you to do this. But is it possible that you could come identify the body?" Just hearing him referred to as 'the body' didn't set well with me. A lump formed in my throat and I could feel myself about to cry again, but I managed to keep it together.

"Yes, yes I can do that." Watching my boss stand there, I quietly ended the call and waited for the bad news that I just knew was coming.

"Is everything alright, Peyton?" she asked. As I looked at her, I realized there was no way I could get out of this with an, "I'm fine." She'd know that I was lying, since she was staring into the depths of my soul already. But for the first time since I'd heard the news, I let the words slip from my mouth. Hearing someone else say them was a lot different than saying them for myself.

"My big brother, Dante... They found him. I mean,   they   found   his   body."

Chapter Thirteen

"IF I SAID THE WORDS,"

PRINCETON JAMES PARRISH.

A week later...

I had really been slacking with visiting my mom but now since I didn't have any other distractions, I woke up with no excuse. She usually wasn't coherent enough to hold a conversation with me while I was there anyways, but she knew I was there and that's all that mattered to me. Just like when I was younger, her presence alone had the power to make me feel better. Walking into the nursing home, I signed myself in and then went to her room where she was pushing a forkful of eggs back and forth on her plate.

I'd brought a bouquet of tropical flowers, knowing that they were her favorite and certain to put a smile on her face if I couldn't. Though my mom had been completely nonverbal for over fifteen years, since a bad batch of drugs lead to a mental breakdown, but she could still get her point across by pointing and babbling meaninglessly.

"How's my favorite girl doing this morning?" I asked, trying to make my mom smile. I could tell that she was mad at me because she turned her head and refused to make eye contact with me. I usually was the only visitor who ever came to see her and even though I'd asked KJ to come visit her while I was locked away, I could tell that he hadn't by the way that she was acting. I glanced at the nurse, who watched us sympathetically. I could sense that she was about to deliver some not-so-good news.

"Mr. Parrish, I think it's time that you consider putting your mom in hospice care. Ms. Vera is regressing every day… She is starting to lose her appetite, she fights us just to get her to take meds… she just sits in bed all day and stares out of the window. Her health is starting to decline and I don't believe that we can care for her the way that she needs.'" Shaking my head, I just knew that they were wrong. I went and sat down on the bed next to my mom, even though she was doing her best to ignore me. That's when I pulled the flowers from behind my back and watched as her eyes lit up. I handed them to her and she inhaled them, smiling. Then I remembered that I had another small present for her. Pulling out my phone, I found the video I saved and put the full screen on so that she would be able to see it.

"Look, mom. It's Ky." Watching my youngest sister and her daughter had my mom cheesing from ear to ear. I gave her a small hug when I watched a single tear fall down her cheek. "It's alright... I promise I'll bring them to see you soon. Ky had to work this morning." I explained. Seeing how her face changed, I knew I had to do something. My father had put her in here and he paid for her care every month, but I didn't care about any of that. I had to do something, because she wasn't living right in that place. The nurse over my mom's care stood in the corner so I turned her.

"Can you get the necessary paperwork?" I could tell the nurse that I was actually thinking about putting my mom there. I'd seen my grandpa in hospice when I was little and that place was cold and fucked up. The only way my mom would ever have to be in there if there was no breath left in my body. She left the room and I pulled the covers off of my mom. I wanted to make sure she got breakfast before we left but when she spit out the eggs on the plate, I tasted it. Not only was it cold, it had the texture of rubber and I quickly spit it out as well. "Don't worry, ma. I'm going to get you out of here and get us some real food." That got a smile out of her and she began to point and clap, just as her nurse and someone who appeared to be her boss came into the room.

"Mr. Parrish, you're ready to start the process of placing your mom in hospice care? I understand how difficult this must be for you but I promise we're going to make this as quick and easy as possible. Okay?" she asked, talking to me like I was a kid. She usually dealt with my father so I knew she was skeptical but nobody cared more about my mom's wellbeing then me. I watched as she and the nurse exchanged glances but I didn't let them know that I'd noticed. That's when I turned to them and made sure that they understood my next words very carefully.

"You guys aren't transferring my mom to hospice, you're discharging her. She's coming home to be with me, where she belongs. I'll call someone about getting in-home care for her around the clock, but you have lost your goddamn mind if you think that I'm going to allow you to just let her sit around and rot." I could tell that they both had questions, but I wasn't listening to any of that. She could tell I wasn't budging so she quickly went through the paperwork with me. I could tell that she didn't want to release her, especially since my dad was the one paying for her to be there, but after I signed a quick check for a five-figure amount, she quickly agreed. After reading the paperwork over, I quickly signed it so that we could get out of there. I'll admit, I had no clue what I was doing but this was my mom. So whatever I had to do, I would do it with no questions asked.

As soon as I packed my mom's clothes up and got her into the car, I realized that I was running low on groceries at home and wouldn't have much for my mom to eat. I'd just gotten out two weeks ago and had been eating fast food ever since. Without Peyton and Taylen around, there was no need to fill up a whole refrigerator full of groceries. I'd tried to keep my mind busy but at moments like this, I really missed her. Sighing, I pulled out my phone and quickly ordered groceries so that I could just pick them up, get home and cook. I wasn't the best, but I could do a little something. Then I pulled out of the parking lot and we headed to the store.

Ordering groceries online made the process easier so we were headed back to my house in no time. It was a new vibe to have my mom in my home, especially since we hadn't been under the same room for almost two decades. I knew it wouldn't be easy but I was her son. She gave me life, so in return I was going to give her the best life that I could, for as long as I could. After I started cooking, I quickly sent a group text to my brother and sisters, knowing that the only thing that could put a bigger smile on my mom's face then everything that had happened today was having all of her kids under one roof. Just like I thought, all of them texted back almost immediately, confirming that they'd be on their way soon. In the meantime, I finished cooking and within a half an hour, Angelina had arrived. Soon after that my baby sister and niece arrived. We all sat around and laughed, joking around like we did when we were younger while we waited on KJ.

When he finally walked in an hour later, his entire vibe was off but I didn't want to mention it around everyone while we were having a good time. Even my mom was interacting in her own way and it made me smile to see that she was finally happy. Kylani, my niece, was enjoying her grandma and had yet to leave her lap since the moment they arrived, but my mom didn't seem to mind. Meanwhile, I was stuck between trying to be the perfect host and make sure everyone was having a good time and keeping an eye on KJ. The entire time that he'd been in the house he had yet to say more than four words to anybody. Even now, he was sitting in the corner, isolating himself from everyone else. I brought him a beer and he ignored me. When I finally got into the kitchen, he came in behind me and motioned for me to follow him outside. I was confused but I did what he said. "What's up, bro? What's wrong?" I asked as I watched him light up a cigarette, I knew something was up. After smoking since he was nineteen years old, KJ gave up smoking after almost seven years. That's how I knew something serious was going on, but he still wasn't saying anything. He finally managed to look me in my eyes and then dropped the cigarette onto the ground, crushing it with his shoe.

"PJ... I was picking up a client from the airport this morning for dad, and..." I could tell that he was struggling to find his words. Even though staring at him probably didn't make it any better, KJ was starting to make me nervous.

"Okay, and? What are you trying to say? Spit it out. Damn." That's when he finally got the nerve he needed and took a deep breath in.

"I saw Peyton." My eyes nearly bugged out of my head as I made sure that I wasn't being punked, despite the sore spot he knew that I had for Peyton and Taylen.

"I looked everywhere for her. Are you sure? Maybe it was just someone who looked like Peyton." That's when he showed me a photograph he'd taken and my breath caught in my throat. It was definitely

Peyton and baby girl. I was relieved to see that they were okay, but the anger I felt was only starting to get worse. In my head, she was becoming too good at abandoning me. Still, I could tell that my brother still had something to say so I remained quiet and observed everything happening around me. I watched KJ's adam's apple stay lodged in his throat. I knew it was bad.

"There's something else." I couldn't imagine what else he had to say, so I sat there and waited until he continued talking.

"She looked sick... Like really sick."

"Sick how? Like cancer sick? What do you mean, Kingston?" I shot question after question out, because honestly, my mind was running a hundred miles a second. Even after everything we'd been through and how betrayed she made me feel, there was nobody I loved in the world like Peyton and something happening to her would break my heart. Kingston shrugged and my heart dropped. But still, I knew that I had to do something.

Chapter Fourteen

"NO ONE FEELS THE SAME."

KINGSTON COLBY PARRISH, JR.

Earlier that day...

I hit my vape pen repeatedly as I waited for my father's clients to exit the airport. I was confused as to why he couldn't get one of our drivers to do it, since that's what they were paid for but I kept my mouth shut regardless. Since they were international clients, I figured it had something to do with their culture so I didn't question him. In waiting there for over an hour though, I was starting to feel like some sort of punk.

Continuously watching the door, my window was rolled all the way down so that my car could air out, which allowed me to be observant of everything going on around me. That's why my jaw dropped when I saw Peyton come out of the airport entrance, I couldn't believe my eyes. Even from hundreds of yards away though, something didn't look right. Despite everything that had gone down and even with the grimy shit she had done,

Peyton looked thin and frail. Something didn't look right and part of me couldn't help but wonder if she was on drugs. I thought about getting out of the car to approach and ask her why she played Princeton the way that she did, but before I could, it was like she could sense me. The moment that I opened the door of my car and stepped out, she turned around and looked dead at me. Before I could stop her, she booked it around the corner and I lost my visual of her. I knew that was my sign to let it go. I didn't even chase my own women, so chasing after Peyton wasn't an option. However, I just wanted to make sure her and the baby were okay. I had a soft spot for the baby, because she was innocent in this equation.

The more that I sat there waiting for my father's clients, the more impatient I became and my mind started to roam aimlessly, so I pulled up to the other side of the pick-up lot in case they had been waiting out there for me all along. God showed all the way out too because Peyton was standing right there, clearly waiting for her ride. Since I was behind her, she didn't see me and so I snuck up to her. That way, there was no running this time.

"Where you been at?" I asked, skipping all the formalities as she turned around like she'd been caught shoplifting. Usually, I tried to stay out of my siblings' lives, especially when it came to love, but Peyton had done my brother so bad, I couldn't just ignore that. Before our eyes even met, tears were already welling up in hers.

"K.J, I can explain..." she cried, before I raised my hand to stop whatever sob story was about to come my way.

"Explain what? Why you broke my brother's heart? Peyton, Princeton loved you... He had genuine love for you and wanted to do whatever to make sure you and your baby were good. I didn't see you as that type of girl but you really left him hanging. That's some fucked up shit you pulled. I can't trust anything you have to say... Wherever you were at, you should have stayed there." I never considered myself a fucked up person but even I wasn't expecting my words to come out so harsh. It hadn't sounded so cold while they were inside my head. Peyton's face broke and I could tell that she wanted to cry but held it together. I turned around to go back to my car, but then she called after me. Despite how pissed off I was, I turned back around because I wanted to see wht would say.

"You don't trust me... and you have every right not to, but I didn't leave Princeton because I wanted to. I had to." I was about to continue our conversation since it seemed she had a lot to tell me but then a car pulled up and she had loaded her daughter and her inside, too quickly for me to say anything. But then, she got back out and waved over to me. "Can you please not say anything to your dad or Princeton? Please? I'm not trying to start anything." She pleaded. I nodded in agreement, but the wheels inside my head were already turning and my brain was telling me that my dad had something to do with this. I needed to talk to PJ about this, but I knew that would start something so I decided to talk to my dad first.

Something about Peyton's last words to me struck me as odd, but they played over and over in my head. After finally picking up my father's clients like I was supposed to, I took them to the office. They headed in and I waited outside, until I decided not to anymore. I knew he was in a meeting but I greeted his secretary and then walked in, making it seem like I was checking in even though I wasn't. In reality, I was just assessing the situation and deciding the best time to confront him about my suspicions. I sat in on the meeting until Princeton sent me a text, with our mother's picture attached and I couldn't help but smile. Knowing she was home removed a lot of stress from our lives, and I visibly relaxed while my dad pitched his idea to all of his comrades. Luckily for me, he was close to finishing so I didn't interrupt. I didn't say shit until after everyone had left the room. My dad knew I was in the room, because he had watched me come in but he had headed towards the window after the meeting and hadn't turned back around since. It was clear that he didn't have the balls to do it, so I started the conversation.

"You know, dad... I always try to give you the benefit of the doubt since you are my father and the reason that I am the man that I am. But every time I try to prove that you're a good man with a good heart, you do some off the wall, outlandish shit." I spat, walking over the door to lock it so that one of my dad's annoying ass employees couldn't interrupt this much-needed conversation. That's when I finally got my dad's attention and he spun around, watching me like he had fire dancing in his eyes. Then that mean ass look vanished and a smile replaced it.

"What are you preaching about now, Jr.?" I watched him for a moment, wishing I had a way to knock that stupid smile right off his face. Then I figured out how to do it without ever laying a hand on him.

"That little plan of yours didn't work. Peyton is back." This time, it was my turn to be entertained while his face fell and his jaw basically dropped to the ground. "Whatever it is that you did, you better work on fixing it. Everyone can tell Princeton is in love with that girl and you getting in the way of that if just going to make him hate you."

Chapter Fifteen

"NOBODY IS WATCHING,"

SHONDAE LATRELLE MASON.

5 ½ weeks prior…

The interaction with Princeton Parrish hadn't gone the way my mom wanted and the whole situation with Peyton and my niece was starting to drive my mom crazy and even though there were times when I was younger that I questioned my mom's sanity, there was no longer any question about it. My mom, Shondell Laren Mason was out of her damn mind. I watched as she had two men drag Princeton's ex into the house we were renting while we were in town and throwing her onto the floor beside the couch. She was face down in the carpet but by the way that she was moaning and groaning, I could tell that she was in a lot of pain.

Motioning for one of them to come to the computer, she started up her laptop and plugged the camera in. With a few clicks of the keys and a few helpful pointers from my mom, one of the men quickly accomplished whatever it was that my mom desired, I could tell by the wicked look on her face. I was confused so I stood around and watched. But when the woman on the floor finally managed to flip herself onto her back, I gasped. Bile ran to the back of my mouth as I rushed to the bathroom, trying to get that visual image in my head out, to no avail. When I finally made it back outside, I could hear my mom talking to someone frantically. Yet, I got to the living room and she was standing there calmly. That's when I realized what was happening as I pieced two and two together. She was lying to the police to get Princeton locked up for whatever she had done to his ex. When I looked on the laptop, completely photo-shopped pictures of Princeton smacking the woman in public were on there. I wanted no parts of anything that was about to happen so I ran out of the house as fast I could, ignoring my mom when I heard her call my name vigorously. When I was sure that she didn't have any of her guys chasing me, I stopped running. But then, I got a second idea. I couldn't do much if I ran away because I knew nothing about Cleveland, but if I went back and watched, pretending to be the obedient daughter my mom wanted me to be, it would be easy to get all the information I needed in order to help Peyton out. If I did that, she would have to protect me from the wench I called my mother.

Turning back towards the house my mom and I were renting while we were in town, I calmed myself down and sat on the steps until I felt my lungs starting to operate normally again. When I walked back into the house, my mom had barely noticed I was gone and hardly spared me a second glance as she continued on with her sinister plan and while I sat quiet, pretending to be compliant with everything going on, I secretly pulled my phone out and began audio recording. As long as I didn't make eye contact with my mom, she wouldn't know anything was up but I was so focused on staring at the screen on my phone that I hadn't even realized one of the dudes helping my mom was watching me. Every time we'd meet eachother's gaze, he'd either wink at me or look away and it was starting to make me nervous. Something didn't feel right, but I hesitated to say anything. Instead, I relied my attention on making sure that I kept my hand steady and calm.

Everything seemed to go fine. My mom finished her psychotic antics and then headed to bed, per her usual. That's when I put on my hoodie and waited until everything was calm again. When I was pretty sure that she was sleeping, I headed out. I made it to the door and nearly screamed when someone was on the other side of the door. That's when I ran right into a hard, muscular body and tried not to scream. Instead of a loud scream like what I imagined in my head, my voice caught in my throat and it came out like a sick whimper of a cat. Usually, I would have laughed at myself but looking into Perry's eyes, the flirtatious, handsome man from earlier, I was too scared to do even that. He was no longer winking at me but instead had the meanest smile I'd ever seen on a real person before.

"Going somewhere?" he asked and before I could muster up a lie, I could hear my mom approaching behind me. I knew it was her because she had a bad habit of not picking up her feet when she walked. The dragging drove me crazy.

"And I thought I could trust my own daughter..." Spinning around, instead of sinking to my feet like the melting wicked witch, I could feel my courage rising three feet taller.

"I want no parts of this. I want out and you're going to give it to me or I'm going to release information that will everyone questioning you." For once, she didn't argue with me once.

Chapter Sixteen

"LET ME BLEED YOUR LOVE AWAY."

PRINCETON JAMES PARRISH.

To say that I didn't feel some type of way about what Kingston said, would've been a lie. Peyton pissed me and maybe even broke my heart, that was for sure but I never wanted anything bad to happen to her or her baby, so when I heard that she was struggling and maybe not doing so well, my stomach began to feel queasy. So even while the rest of my family was sitting around and laughing, my mind was on an entirely different level. An entirely different dimension actually. KJ sat across from me on the couch, watching me the entire time and even though I never looked his way, I could tell that his eyes never left me. My train of thought was going in no particular direction but yet, it still managed to circle aimlessly around Peyton. What she was doing, how she was doing, who she was with and why they weren't protecting her… the list was endless inside my head. It became so bad that I started to cradle my head in my hands. Angelina was the first one to notice that my vibe was off.

"Are you alright, PJ?" she asked and I felt everyone look at me. Even my mom was trying to figure out what was going on, in her own, silent way. I knew that my brain wouldn't relax until I got the answers that I needed and it seemed that my big brother already knew what was up because the moment I stood up, he held out his car keys for me to take. I looked at him, giving him a stare that confirmed he was giving me permission to drive his baby, his all black Audi A-4. He just laughed.

"Dawg, I know you like the back of my hand. Go figure this shit out with your girl so you can stop walking around like a lost puppy dog." Usually, I would've sat there and argued with him but my mind was on Peyton and getting to wherever she was. First though, I knew that something more important needed to be handled first. Everything hung in the balance of that. Finally snatching the keys out of my brother's hand, I marched out of the door with one thing on my mind. Once I made it into the car, I realized how stupid I looked because I literally had no clue where my dad was- until I remembered that he'd emailed me a copy of his agenda for the day. I made it to my office's luxury downtown office in about twenty minutes, which even surprised me because the traffic was crazy. But I drove like a madman into the parking garage and then barged my way into my father's conference room. He seemed to be caught off guard but he wasn't shocked, and that made me nervous.

"Why'd you do it? I mean, damn... I've never been the best son in your opinion, but I've never treated you even close to the way you treat me..." My dad started to click his tongue like I was annoying him. I waited for him to reprimand me, because I knew it was coming just by his posture but just like he did constantly when he was in deep thought, my father just continued to watch out of the window.

"You know, Princeton... I always knew you'd have the same spirit as your mother..." he began to explain. "Persuasive, emotional..." he started to walk over to where I was standing as I froze like someone was drawing a portrait of me. I had never been scared of my dad before, but this look was nothing like I'd ever seen before either. I found myself feeling like that nine-year old kid getting scolded again. Yet, I did my best to hide it as my heart began to race. "Weak." He spat finally, the words coming out of his mouth so venomous that I fought not to wince. "I hated that about her and you're turning out the exact same way." There were a lot of things that I could and would tolerate, but the disrespect of my mother was not one of those things and I stepped forward, eliminating the gap of space between us before I could even control myself. It took a lot for me to get angry, but all of a sudden, I found myself ready and willing to knock my dad's teeth down his throat. Even in front of all of his people.

"The only thing that my mom was ever weak for, was loving your punk ass. Even when you gave her every reason not to." I responded, looking my dad dead in the eyes. "My mom gave you chance after chance... But I'm less like her than you think. Stay the fuck away from me... and when I find my girls, stay away from them too." I warned as I made my way to the door. Then I heard my dad walking quickly and I turned around to make sure he wasn't trying to hit me in the back of my head and catch me off guard, or something.

"You think that gold-digger and that bastard baby care about you? I just want you to be your best! She left you at your worst!" By no means did I consider myself a light-skinned nigga but I knew all my color had rushed to my face because I could feel the heat rising to my cheeks as I witnessed our argument starting to gather an audience. I didn't care though. Before my dad could say anything else, my hand was gripped around his throat. A decade ago, I wouldn't have even dared but my father wasn't the same, invincible Kingston Sr. that he used to be.

"I don't know who the fuck you think you are, but you will not disrespect Peyton or Taylen like that. Not in my presence. Do you understand?" I seethed. I could tell that he nodded just to get me off him but that didn't stop me from releasing him and watching while he gasped for air. I didn't know I was going to react so bad and that kind of anger wasn't like me so it was time for me to remove myself from the situation. After I finally managed to confront my dad, I felt better and quickly pulled out of the parking garage of my father's empire before building security could catch up with me. I knew that I now needed to catch up with Peyton, but I had no idea how and then, fate intervened. Just as I was about to call my brother, I drove past Grace Hospital and instantly slammed on my brakes, making sure that I wasn't imagining things. But then I saw it. Even from far away I saw it. It was the long tail of the dragon that started at Peyton's neck and worked its way down a path of flowers to her hips. I recognized that tattoo anywhere because I spent so much time tracing over it with my fingers after we made love. I could tell that something was wrong by the way that she was bent over, so I pulled over to see if I could help her.

"Peyton! Hey! Are you alright?" I called. She jumped, definitely surprised to see me. I was expecting her to run, to scream, to do something to avoid me... But she didn't. Instead, she looked up at me and whispered four words that had my stomach falling to my knees.

"No, I'm not. I think I'm pregnant."

Chapter Seventeen

"TAKE ALL MY LOVE."

PEYTON TAHJ EVER.

Uttering the words out of my mouth made it real as hell and the more I thought about it, the more I continued to cry. Being an almost nineteen-year old single mother of one was hard enough, but two? That idea was unimaginable. Therefore, once Princeton got me in the car and cleaned me up, I could tell we were both stuck in our thoughts, both trying to figure out the next step. Princeton nervously gripped the gear but when I reached for his hand, he pulled away. I understood why, but it didn't mean it hurt any less. Just by the look in his eyes, I could tell that he was really done with me and that hurt more than anything, but it wasn't like I didn't deserve it. Pulling my hand back into my lap, I bit down on my bottom lip as I struggled not to cry. Princeton turned the radio up and I watched out of the window as the entire world whizzed by with no idea that my world had just stopped momentarily.

It took him stopping at a red light to even acknowledge my existence.

"So what made you come back? You want me to take care of another kid that's not mine?" My jaw dropped and it was a good thing that his foot was already on the brake because had he not already braced himself for it, the force of my slap might have caused us to get an accident. He rubbed his jaw and shook his head, but whatever else he was about to say, it was clear he wasn't going to and I wasn't trying to hear it. I was already three seconds away from telling him to pull over and let me and my baby out of the car. He must have saw my lips begin to shake because almost immediately, he recognized the mistake of letting those words come out of his mouth. "Pey..." he said, slowly reaching for my hand. This time, I pulled it away. "Peyton, I'm sorry. I didn't mean that."

"Never in a million years did I *ever* expect your help. Let's get that clear. I didn't even come here to see you. I came to identify my brother's cold, dead body. So don't think that I'm here scheming, for whatever reason. I'm not. You can be around if you choose and if you want to go ghost, that's not anything I'm not used to already, anyways... I'll continue to do what I've *been* doing... grinding my ass off." I snapped. I could tell I'd hurt his feelings, but so? He'd hurt mine by insinuating I'd even mention being pregnant if it was another man's baby.

"I mean... don't you think you should take a pregnancy test first? You don't even know, for sure..."

"Trust me, I know. I've had a baby before, Princeton. My body feels the exact same that it did when I first found out I was having Taylen... I'm a woman. I know myself and I know my body and I don't feel normal. Whenever I do go to the doctor, they're going to tell me what I already know. I'm pregnant." Realizing that he had every reason to not believe me, I relaxed and calmed my tone. "But yes... I already know. My doctor's appointment is in three days... back *home* in Arizona." Princeton's entire face changed, but I had no control over that. My life needed to resume after I made sure everything was lined up for my brother's burial. When my life did manage to continue on, it would be in Arizona. My job was there, my life was there and I was tired of being that unstable mom. I promised Taylen and myself that I would stop with all the consistent moving and finally settle down somewhere.

"Okay... so what do we plan on doing about that? It's going to be hard going back and forth for you, and I can't be a deadbeat. That's not in me, you know that. Besides... all the constant flying can't be good for the baby." Reaching over, he placed his hand on my stomach. "I hope it's a girl." He confessed, shocking the hell out of me. "I'd name her Peace." Though Peace Parrish didn't sound good at all to me, I kept my mouth shut. I was just happy to see that he planned on being involved in our baby's life.

"I already have a girl... I want a little boy who looks like me... I always told myself I'd name him Preston." I could look at him and tell that he was repeating it in his head over and over, making sure that it flowed off the tongue easily.

"I have a better idea. If it's a boy.... Why don't we name him Tahj Preston? That way, your family name still continues on. I mean, since our child will have my last name." My jaw dropped. Was he not even going to bring up hyphenating our last names as a possibility?

"What we're not about to do is pretend like I'm not the one doing all the work. Like I don't play a significant part in this... Why can't the baby have both of our names?" He began to mutter something incoherently, but I wasn't going for that. "Speak up. Whatever you have to say, say it. We're too grown for that." When he rubbed his hands over his face, I instantly prepared myself to get pissed off. But then he surprised me.

"Because for starters, before our baby is born... a couple of things need to happen. We need to go to the doctor and make sure you're actually pregnant. Then, you'll need to have my last name." Princeton said it so casually that I thought he was joking, but his face was completely serious. When he looked over at me, his smile melted my heart and my panties.

"Yeah, we'll see." I was preparing for him to drop the subject , but I felt him grab my hand and then kiss on my palm, paying special attention to my ring finger. I could feel my eyes getting heavy but by the time I was about to shut my eyes and take a nap for a moment, we were pulling into Princeton's driveway. When we got out, he grabbed Taylen's car seat and my bags. When he unlocked the door, I was surprised to see his place looked a lot different. But then again, we weren't even in the same house as before. "New decorations huh?" I asked, admiring the place. He walked into the other room to get Taylen situated and then I sat at the kitchen island. A lot of the space on his wall was dedicated to pictures of his family, his mother, KJ and his sisters but there were a lot of evident spaces where pictures had obviously been taken down. Princeton barely paid me any mind when he ventured back to the kitchen and peered through the refrigerator.

"Yeah. I needed a change." He mumbled as he pushed everything back and forth on the refrigerator shelves before deciding on what he wanted to eat. He hadn't bothered to ask me, but that was fine. I was starving so I'd eat anything, but that didn't mean I wanted to eat in silence.

"Why'd you move?" I asked curiously, grabbing an orange out of the basket as I began to peel it.

"I had plans, but things change." He answered simply. The excited Princeton who only wanted to talk about our baby was gone. The cold, careless Princeton was back in his place but I wasn't letting it go that easy.

"Plans for what?" I asked, receiving no answer. "Whose pictures did you take down?" I questioned again. It seemed like he was ignoring me, but then he slammed a cabinet door and nearly scared the hell out of me.

"Don't you get it, Peyton? This house was for you... For us and our family. I had plans for us, Peyton... but you broke my heart."

Chapter Eighteen

"WHEN YOU'RE GONE."

KINGSTON COLBY PARRISH, SR.

Yes, I was still legally married but that didn't mean I couldn't have fun on the side. The satisfaction of my marriage had left long ago, after my youngest was born. Now that my wife was in a home that would better suit her needs, I had to get off somehow. You could judge me if you wanted to, but you'd be wasting your time.

When Jersey emerged from my lap, my children lying rampant on her bottom lip, I felt no type of remorse for "betraying" Princeton. Yes, he was my son. But the lines of loyalty had long been crossed for Princeton and it only took for someone to backstab me once for me to cut off all ties. That even included my blood relatives. Even though a part of me knew I was wrong, there was something about Jersey that I liked. I could see why my son stayed with her for so long. Not only was Justice just average, unlike the trophy girlfriend PJ had now, she was loyal. Princeton's new girlfriend knew that she was beautiful and that was the problem. You could never put pretty bitches in their place because in their mind, they could always find someone better. Jersey was the opposite. She was a bit whiny for my taste, but she knew her role and she played it well. She was submissive and did just as I asked her. So after I had my fill, I put her in line to be the next heir of the Parrish inheritance. Then they both messed it up. Just like everything else, I had to fix it.

Wiping the corners of her mouth, Jersey looked up at me with those big brown eyes and that big pouty look and I felt my irritation rising. I just knew that she was about to ask me for something so I prepared myself to pull out my checkbook.

"Daddy, when are you going to take Jaxx to one of your family gatherings? Don't you think he's old enough now? He needs to meet your family, *his* family..." I knew she was going to mention that little boy again and that was a quick way to ruin my mood. Pushing her the furthest away from me that she would go, I looked out of the window as I pondered my words and the right way to say it.

"Jersey, when that situation first arrived, I told you to take care of it. If my son didn't want a baby by you, why would I?"

My words sounded harsh, but I just needed a scape goat. I'd messed up. In a small timeframe of carelessness, I'd slept with Jersey. When she came to me claiming she was pregnant with *my* child, I did what any hard-working, dedicated family man would do. I threw a bunch of hundred-dollar bills in her face and told her to handle it. I was almost fifty years old. What would it look like for me popping out another child, whose mother wasn't my wife? Too many people would have too many questions. What I didn't have, was time for that. Fortunately for me, I knew exactly how to shut her up. Leaning over to grab her hand, I kissed it softly after making sure it wasn't the same hand that she had just jerked me off with. I knew that I'd have to suck up to her because whether I admitted it or not, I needed Jersey more than she needed me. I needed her companionship and her cooperation. But most importantly, I needed Jersey's silence. Sucking my teeth in annoyance, I opened my checkbook and wrote her ass a check. A little bit of money would keep her distracted enough to keep her off my back. At least for a little while.

Kissing her forehead, I ripped the check out and handed it to her. Her eyes bulged, but little did she know that was going to be the last piece of silent change she was going to get from me for awhile. This situation was about to even itself out. When she hugged my neck, I patted her waist to signal to her that it was time for her to get off of me. That's when she looked at me with sad eyes and I tried to hide my annoyance. "What is it, Jersey? What's wrong now?" I prepared for her to tell me she needed more money, but then she slid her body away from me.

"I know that you don't want me around, Kingston. You have just been using me to get back at Princeton for whatever you feel like he's doing to you. I want no parts of you ruining his life. I love Princeton and I always will. I was wrong for approaching you the way I did, but I was just trying to hurt him the way he hurt me when he dropped me off at that appointment at the clinic. But I was wrong and I won't make excuses for it. I'm going to use this money and I'm going to get the hell out of here. I'm going to go to school and I'm going to make something of myself. For me and my son. You won't ever have to worry about us again." After saying that, she got out of the car and walked away. She stopped mid-stride and turned around to look at me before walking to her car. That's when I knew... I really would never see her again. I was relieved to say the least, but I also couldn't help but wonder what trouble would come along with that.

Chapter Nineteen

"HOW YOU GOT ME NOW."

PEYTON TAHJ EVER.

I didn't know what else to say to Princeton. 'I'm sorry' didn't seem adequate enough. 'Give me another chance' seemed to jump the gun, but I needed him to know how important he was to me. How important he was to Taylen. Watching her eyes light up seeing him, even after all this time, gave me all the confirmation I needed. They didn't share the same DNA, but Princeton was Taylen's father in every way imaginable. I knew that I had to make Princeton believe me, no matter what I had to do. His back was still turned to me but when I wrapped my arms around his waist, he turned to face me. The eye contact was all I needed.

"Princeton, there's nothing and nobody I want more in this world than you. There's nothing I wouldn't do to prove that." That seemed to get his attention and he picked me up, his hands never leaving my stomach.

"Do you mean that?" he asked, skeptically. I nodded without hesitating.

"With everything inside of me." I confessed

honestly. He surprised me and left the room, but came back almost instantly.

"Then prove it, Peyton." He challenged me. I know that he could tell that I was confused. Honestly, I was bewildered until he got down on one knee. "I wanted to wait until I could give you this big ceremony with cameras all around, catching the moment you agree to be my wife... But, fuck it. All that it has ever been is me and you, so we're the only two people who matter to me right now. I've never been the man to play hide and seek. Not when it's something I crave... Like you. Will you be my wife, Peyton Tahj Ever? Will you make me the happiest man on earth?" My heart fluttered and my words weren't even coming out properly so I nodded my head vigorously. Once he slid the ring onto my finger, he pulled me into his arms and I cried as he kissed me and wiped my tears away at the same time. I couldn't help but fear for the future. After all, I'd never been the best judge of character... But something about this, with Prince, just felt right to me. It felt like the most natural thing in the world to love him. I knew it was just my doubts, but I had one very important question to ask him.

"Why do you want me to marry you, Princeton? Is it because I'm having your baby? People have kids together all the time without being married, you know…" This question seemed to irritate him more and he sighed, pulling me into his lap in one quick motion. He kissed my lips between every word he spoke.

"Peyton, I'd be lying if I said the thought of you having my kid didn't both scare and excite the hell out of me at the same time… But believe me when I say, I want to marry you because you're *you*. We've been through a lot of shit, but there's nobody I'd rather do this with than you." That seemed to be all I needed to hear because before long, we were all over each other like horny teenagers. It was a good thing that Taylen was in the other room because our clothes were off in moments. I understood what he meant by craving someone's presence. Every second I was away, I thought about Princeton and what he was doing, who he was with… I wasn't too grown to admit that I was stupid. Stupid for not talking to Princeton about his dad and everything that was going on, but that mistake would never happen again.

Our conversation came to an abrupt end when my phone began to ring relentlessly and I glanced at it, taking a moment to try to calm the knot developing in my throat. My anxiety shot through the roof and Princeton watched me closely as he glanced between me and my phone. "Do you need me to get that?" I shook my head and quickly picked up the phone, my anxiety shooting through the roof as I watched the number flash across my screen. Just by the area code, I knew it was my parents returning my call. I'd been calling them ever since I arrived to share the news about Dante.

"H-hello?" I stammered. Just by the area code, I knew it was my parents returning my call, but I had suddenly lost all my courage. Having this conversation wasn't easy, but it needed to be done. Since I knew nothing would help ease the band-aid off, I decided to just spit it out. It was clear that neither of my parents had listened to the voicemail, which meant they had no idea who they were calling back. "It's Peyton. I was just calling you about Dante. I know you two probably won't believe me... but he's dead." Swallowing my words hardly, I closed my eyes and could practically witness my parents' faces behind my eyelids. I was starting to get upset slowly, which I knew because I could feel the heat rising up my body, but I tapped my finger on the table as I counted down in my head. For the sake of my baby, I had to manage my emotions. The exact same way I did when I was younger. Nobody really knew it, but my parents hadn't always been this cold to me. My mom had been my best friend at one point. I wasn't sure of the straw that broke the camel's back, but our bond experienced a turn-around point when my parents found out I was with Talon, the neighborhood delinquent. They hated his mom and everything about him and looking back at it, I probably should have listened. But if I had done that, I would never have gotten my princess. I assumed my parents were just being overprotective of me. Little did I know, I didn't even know the half of it.

The silence hovering on the other end of the line haunted me as if I were staring at a ghost, but I was too scared to say something. Honestly, even if it was just them being quiet, I was glad to have them around. "Mom? Dad? Did you hear me?" I questioned, my voice cracking like I was a little girl in trouble again. I hadn't spoken to them since announcing to them that I was pregnant with my first child at the age of eighteen and although I wanted to do nothing more than catch them up, and tell them all I had accomplished, I knew now wasn't the time for that. They had practically disowned me and by the lack of contact, I could only imagine that they still felt the same way. After all, what kind of parents went a year without even checking up on their daughter to make sure she was alive? I had been on my own and in my heart, I knew that it would continue to be that way. I never had a mother to show me how to rock Taylen to sleep when she was inconsolable, but I learned. I had turned into a damn good mom without the help of my own and that was okay with me. In the end, I realized I had never been alone. God sent me Princeton to help nurse the pain away.

My parents being absent from my daughter's and I's

lives hurt, but the silence that they were giving me only made things hurt worse. Everyone knew how close Dante and I were. Only ten months apart, we got into so much trouble together that our parents eventually gave up on trying to separate us. We'd grown up around each other every day, in the same class. There was hardly a time that you saw my brother without me. But all that changed when I was fifteen. Dante started freaking out, hanging out and doing hardcore drugs. Things stronger than just weed. Basically, my big brother wasn't my brother any more. A year later, he was diagnosed with schizophrenia but instead of things getting better because we received the answers we were seeking, things only managed to get worse. He refused to take his medicine and eventually, refused to come home at all. We did everything we could, but the law is pretty clear. If he wasn't hurting himself or someone else, there was no way that they could force him to do something he wasn't interested in. That's how we got to this point. I heard my dad clearing his throat, and I prepared myself for the bad news coming my way. He did the same thing every time he was about to say something he knew I wouldn't like.

"Peyton, we have nothing else to say to you. Please stop calling us."

Chapter Twenty

"AFTER BREAKING DOWN MY HEART."

PRINCETON JAMES PARRISH.

Peyton didn't have much to say after our discussion, but it wasn't like there was many words being said between us anyways. After giving her everything she asked for and then some, I watched as she laid in the bed, satisfied. That was fine with me though because the more silence enveloped us, the happier I got. *Peyton and I were going to have a baby.* I said those things about not being her baby's father because I wanted her to feel a small amount of the pain I felt when she up and left me. More than once. But then I realized something. In all of my past relationships, it had been full of "one-ups". Jersey would do something and in an effort to make myself feel better, I'd do something back. But I was done with that. I didn't want my relationship with Peyton to be like that. As the mother of my first biological child, not that biology mattered with Taylen, Peyton *would* be my wife and that meant whatever issues we had, we'd work through them. As a team.

Turning around from the refrigerator when I

heard fast footsteps, I watched Peyton make a bee-line to the bathroom and I quickly followed behind her to make sure that she was alright. I was definitely not prepared for the mess I walked into, literally, but I kept my game face on and did my best not to pass out or throw up with her. There was vomit all over my bathroom floor but I stepped over each puddle like I was a kid again, playing that lava game. Sitting on the edge of the bathtub and secretly dreading cleaning that mess up, I held Peyton's hair up while she gagged mercilessly.

"I'm sorry." Peyton groaned while she dry-heaved, her stomach completely empty at this point. All of her clothes were messed up so when she was done, I stripped her out of everything except her bra and panties. Then I picked her up and took her into the guest bathroom where I ran her a semi-warm bubble bath. I could tell that she was embarrassed, so I stepped outside to call my sister while Peyton got comfortable.

When my younger sister answered the phone, I wasted no time in formalities.

"Hey, Ky... I need morning sickness remedies. Now." I demanded, too intent on cleaning the bathroom to listen to her laugh and gossip with my other sister in the background. She must have sensed that now wasn't the time for her jokes, because she quickly gave me the answer to my question.

"Peppermints, ginger ale... chamomile, lemons... Foods that don't have a strong smell. Crackers... and lukewarm food. Not too hot, not too cold." She told me everything, drilling information into my head. I was glad that she was taking it slow because it took me forever to find a pen and a piece of paper. I quickly wrote everything down that she told me and then hung up the phone, not bothering to say anything. It wasn't until after I heard the dial-tone that I realized I didn't even say thank you. I went back into the guest bathroom to give Peyton a toothbrush and mouthwash and then I went back into the other bathroom to clean it thoroughly. I only got about two minutes in before I threw everything to the side and then called up a cleaning service, who told me they could come immediately. So I made a quick trip to the grocery store, just to pick up the things my sister told me to buy and also buy some stuff for us to eat, but I was in and out of there within ten minutes. I wanted to get back to Peyton and make sure that she was okay. When I made it back into our house, I put everything down when I heard Taylen fussing. But as soon as she saw me, she started cooing and smiling. I quickly changed her and then put her in front of the TV, as I went to go check on Peyton. I found her still in the bathtub. Knocked out. I didn't want her to drown so I quickly grabbed a towel and then pulled her out, not caring that I was now soaked. When I got her on the bed, she started to slightly wake up but I kept drying her off. I stayed focus and put her in one of my clean t-shirts, laughing when I realized she managed to stay asleep the whole time. Kissing her stomach, I went into the other room to watch Taylen even though I wanted to do nothing more than get a second round in with Peyton.

Four hours later, I walked into the bedroom to find Peyton still sleeping and since I couldn't leave Taylen, Kyla agreed to bring me everything I needed to make Peyton feel better. She even agreed not to mention anything to anyone else until we knew for sure, even though I already knew for sure. After worshipping the ground that she walked on from the front and the back, I noticed little subtle changes that I wasn't even sure that she caught.

Chapter Twenty-One

"NO ONE SEES MYSELF LIKE YOU DO."

PRINCETON JAMES PARRISH.

I knew that in order to make Peyton my wife, I needed to get my dad's blessing. If nothing else, I needed him to know that my marriage to Peyton was going to happen regardless of his approval or not. If he refused to accept Peyton, Taylen and the baby we were about to have together, I would just have to remove him from our lives. There was no other option. I was prepared to do whatever it took for my father to realize I was serious. What he didn't know was that I had a secret weapon against him that would change his entire tune.

Nobody but KJ knew about it, and for good reason. KJ and I suspected that if my dad knew that my mom had been in physical and speech therapy four days a week for months and was starting to get her basic functions back, he'd pull some type of card to put her back where she was to begin with. It was starting to feel like we were getting our mom back, or at least the parts we loved about her back. She was the same... but yet she wasn't and I knew that she would never be. Instead of adoring and worshipping my father like she did, she started to shake whenever his name was even mentioned. I couldn't help but think that she'd seen a side of him that nobody else had ever seen. I couldn't prove it but I knew he'd done something to her. I could feel it and once I figured it out, I was determined to get him back for it. Even if that meant ruining his life. Yes, both of our reputations were at stake, but I was young. It was nothing for me to re-build, since I already had access to the list of all of my father's clients. Kingston on the other hand, had spent his entire life working on building Prince & Parrish. A scandal like this would send everything he'd built crumbling down.

Even with that being said, sitting in front of my dad now, a week away from my wedding to the most beautiful woman in the world, was the most terrifying thing in the world. The calm poise he held even in a situation like this wrecked my nerves, but I knew that I had to play his game to get the results I wanted. Instead of running away like a cowardly dog with my tail between my legs, I sat there silently with my hands folded in front of me. To anybody else around us, it looked like a semi-casual business meeting between comrades. If only they knew I was about to have the hardest conversation of my life. If my dad thought I'd shy away from this, he had another thing coming. No matter how anyone felt about the situation at hand, Peyton and Taylen weren't members of my family. They were my family. My sisters, my parents and everybody else in between all had to take a backseat down that we were focusing on bringing a new life into the world. Anybody who couldn't accept their roles in my life, had no room for me in theirs. As much as it would suck to ban my father from my life, anything I needed to do for my peace of mind would just have to be done. Especially if it affected Peyton, Taylen and the new baby in any way. That was no longer an option for me.

I took a long chug of water, in my head pretending that it was Absinthe burning its way down my throat. I nearly swallowed it all in one gulp. Maybe to others I seemed like I was thirsty but once I finished, I thought about flagging the waiter down and ordering an actual shot. There was an awkward silence between me and my father, until I finally managed to gather up the strength to start the conversation. It was time for me to say what I needed to say.

"Look, I know that you and Peyton have had your issues… but, I need to make sure that all of that is past us now. I have plans with her and for her. If you're not for it, then you're against us and I can't have that." I silently gave myself one point when I saw my father's facial expression change. It was no secret that my father had tough skin, so to see that I had that kind of power felt good. I had him right where I wanted him. "Isn't that what you used to tell us? If you're not for the family, you're against us." I questioned, throwing his exact words right back at him. Now that they had a new meaning, it wasn't hard to tell that he wasn't feeling it. Gritting his teeth, he pulled his chair in closer to the table. I guess he didn't want anyone else to hear what he was saying.

"That hoe is not your family and if you turn your back on me for that exploiter, you are not the son that I thought you were. You are not the man that I thought you were. You haven't known her a year. Have I not done enough for you? You are the man that you are, because of me! Don't you ever forget that!" he roared. The discretion of our conversation went out the window because people started staring in our direction. But if it was a show that he wanted, a show is exactly what he would get. Nobody called Peyton out of her name.

Fighting the urge to snatch my father up from the collar, I noticed my knee rocking furiously, as my blood pressure rose in anger but I refused to act a fool. At least not right now. But I had lost my appetite already so I needed to speed up the end of this conversation. Pulling an envelope out of my pocket, I opened all of the documents and pushed them in front of his face.

"You can have all of your lawyers look at it if you want, but everything is intact. The dissolution of our partnership is now complete. I just need your signature so that we can get a court date to separate our assets. I don't and won't ever need your money, so you can keep it. But I've built our client list, so I am not leaving this business relationship without it. Our business relationship is done and as far as I'm concerned, you're right. I'm no longer your son." With that being said, I left the paperwork in front of him for him to look over and then I walked away. Today was a day for new beginnings and leaving old things behind.

"You're making a mistake." He called after me. That alone almost made me laugh, but I was done with the back and forth. Not sparing him a reaction or another word, I continued to walk out.

Chapter Twenty-Two

"WITH YOUR CONSTANT SHAME."

PEYTON TAHJ EVER.

I could tell that Princeton was up to something by the goofy grin on his face but I played along and let him do his thing as he loaded me and Taylen into the car. Supposedly, after our first appointment with our OB-GYN, Princeton had a surprise for me and I couldn't wait to see what it was. He had already surprised me with the house and the proposal so whatever was next, I was ready for.

Our appointment was a pretty standard one. Not much was going to happen this early anyways but because I had already been through pregnancy one time before, I knew what was heading my way. There was nothing the doctor could tell me about my symptoms because it had been the exact same way with Taylen. Princeton on the other hand, you could tell had never been through this. He listened intently while the doctor explained everything, step by step. His amusement with our child was so cute that if I had not been so amazed by every little question he asked, I would have been laughing. But I already knew that he was going to have a slight obsession with our baby because of how he rested his hand on my stomach while we slept. When he kissed me goodnight, I kissed our baby too. He even talked to it and held conversations, despite the fact that I told him our child couldn't hear his voice yet. I had missed out on that experience with Taylen's father and now, I felt grateful. I was about to get my second chance at having the family effect I'd always dreamed of. There was no better feeling and every time I moved my hair out of my face and noticed the rock that rested on my finger, I realized that compared to a lot of other people, I was blessed. Hell, compared to the person I was last year, I was blessed. Not even a year ago, I was in a toxic environment and crying myself to sleep as I tried to find an out for my daughter and I. I just wanted to be happy and I wanted Taylen to be loved. Now, both of my wishes had been fulfilled and I couldn't have been more thrilled.

Thinking about the luck I had and as I watched my soon-to-be husband fawn over the sonogram of our child, I felt tears escape the brim of my eyelids. Even if I had a chance to control them, I wouldn't have. The amount of love I felt was overwhelming. The doctor noticed my tears and quickly handed me a tissue. Princeton on the other hand, had already gotten accustomed to my mood swings and barely paid me any mind. Sometimes, it upset me but watching him show Tay her new little brother or sister was warming my heart. Even the doctor seemed to be enjoying the interaction between father and daughter. Suddenly, I heard Princeton sniffling and when I looked up, it was clear that he was crying. I wanted to call him out, but I refrained. The last thing I wanted him to think was that I was questioning his masculinity. The doctor must have noticed the look on my face because she giggled under her breath and then turned the monitor to the ultrasound machine off.

"Let me print out these pictures for you two, then you can be on your way." She smiled, leaving the room. Apparently, the doctor was the only thing keeping Princeton together because the moment the door shut, Prince lost it... and left me completely confused.

"Prince, are you alright? What's wrong?" I asked, hopping off the table as I pulled my shirt down. Even Taylen seemed to be confused and when I grabbed her from him, she began crying. He sat down and took a deep breath, but clearly couldn't get it together. I sat beside him and rubbed his back until it was clear that he wanted to talk about it.

"I love Taylen to death... You're telling me that I'm going to love someone else like this? More than this?" The confession alone brought tears to my eyes so I did my best to comfort him. But I couldn't help but laugh. He seemed so scared at the changes to come and as was I. Yet, at the same time... I was readier than I had ever been. "I don't want her to feel like I'm replacing her." The sad look that crossed over his face resembled a lost puppy dog so I kissed his cheek, hoping it would make him feel better.

"You won't love this new baby more, Princeton... and I'm sure she will know that she is still the apple of mommy and yours' eyes-,"

"Daddy." He corrected me. I looked up at him in confusion, even though I knew exactly what he was saying. "You said mommy and 'yours'... I'm Taylen's daddy. I may not have created her from my own DNA, but she is mine, nonetheless. I've never felt love like this. Not even with you. No offense." He responded, making me laugh as he made funny faces at Taylen.

"None taken. You're supposed to love my baby

more than you love me. That means you're a real one"
Kissing my cheek, Princeton's eyes never left Taylen and I
couldn't do anything but laugh. Seeing how crazy he was
about my daughter made me curious to see what he'd be
like with the new baby. Truthfully, I couldn't wait. After
receiving our sonogram pictures of our baby, Princeton
grabbed Taylen and we headed back to the car. I still had
no idea where we were going or what he had planned, but
I knew it would be something by the stupid look on his
face.

He watched intently as he drove, occasionally
stealing glances at me as he held my hand. By this point, I
was nervous but Princeton wasn't. I knew that as long as I
was with him, I was safe. Leaning the seat back, I relaxed,
sat back and rubbed my stomach, both of us enjoying the
ride. I didn't realize it, but I was falling asleep and I didn't
wake up until I felt a hand rubbing on my thigh.

"Baby, wake up..." Princeton whispered, kissing on
my neck as my eyes fluttered open and I struggled to get
my vision back in focus. Before I even figured out where
we were, the smell of food hit my nostrils and
immediately made my mouth water.

"How did you know I was hungry?" I asked, getting

out of the car as fast as my legs would let me. Princeton smiled and grabbed Taylen out of the back, since he was adamant that the carseat was too heavy for me to carry in my "condition". His overprotectiveness made me roll my eyes, but I knew his heart was in the right place. Besides, as much as I wanted to be an independent woman, I would gladly accept his help. I'd been doing the single mom thing for so long, I had no idea how to even let someone else take the lead. When he grabbed my hand though, I knew there was something else to this. The look on his face wasn't just a hungry one. It read of mischief and surprise, both of which he was really good at, so I know that I needed to prepare myself for whatever was about to happen.

Then I saw them. Walking us over to the table, my knees buckled and tears flooded my eyes when I realized I was standing right in front of my parents. My dad was a little balder than he had been more than a year ago and my mom was a little grayer, but they both looked the same. Extending his hand, Princeton greeted my father first with a handshake built for a businessman. It was strong, dominant, and most importantly, it obviously got my father's attention because he smiled and I'd never seen him do that with any boy I'd ever talked to. But on the other hand, Princeton was not like any other boy I'd ever dated. Everything about him wreaked "BOSS". From the way that he walked, the way that he talked, and the fact that he liked to wear nice suits even if it was just to go out to eat.

He was a grown man. My mother must have even noticed the change because she stood up and embraced him, as if she'd known him his whole life. All three of them were smiling and I was still distraught. I had no idea what the hell was going on, and after the conversation I'd had on the phone, I didn't think I'd ever hear from my parents again. But now, they were sitting in front of me and I didn't know what to do with myself. The tears came even further when after we all had sat down, I looked up to see my favorite person joining our table. My baby sister, Morgen. She definitely wasn't a baby any more though and when she saw me, she embraced me so hard I felt like the prodigal son. Well, the prodigal daughter. By the time that was finished, there was no dry eyes sitting around our table. I swore I even saw a tear escape Princeton's eyes. But then he got it together and the reason for this meeting was revealed. Clearing his throat, we all sat down and the waitress came right up to take our orders. After this eventful meeting, my stomach was feeling kind of queasy so I didn't go as hard on the menu as I wanted. Instead, I just ordered a bowl of grits and some toast.

My mother broke the ice first. Taking a long sip of her mimosa, she pushed her glass away and then peered over at Taylen, who was still in her car-seat. Then something unexpected happened. When they made eye contact, Taylen smiled at her grandma and my mom immediately began to cry. She reached out for Taylen and Princeton didn't hesitate in handing her over. I couldn't help the tears that escaped my eyes as I watched my mom love on my daughter, completely oblivious to anything else going on around us. That's all I had ever wanted, was for someone to love Taylen the way that I loved her.

"Hi grandma's baby!" she cooed, kissing Taylen all over her cheeks until she squealed. The whole table laughed and that's when Taylen saw my dad. His beard caught her attention and she leaned over into him. After a while, it was like ring around the rosie and my parents and sister took turns holding Taylen, who was interacting with them like she'd known them her entire life. But even though I was glad they were enjoying my baby, there was some other things that we needed to address and watching me as I shifted uncomfortably, it seemed that Princeton was going to speak up for me. But I didn't need him to. I took a deep breath to keep my stomach calm. I knew the one conversation that would kill the mood, but it had to be done. Even though my mom was too busy loving on Taylen to even pay any attention to anything I was saying.

"Mom, I'm really sorry about all that stuff I said before. I didn't mean it." I apologized sincerely. There wasn't a day that passed by where I didn't regret saying all that stuff to the woman who gave me life. After all, if Taylen ever fixed her mouth to talk to me like that, she'd be swallowing her teeth. My mom waved it off, but I wasn't letting it go that easily. "No, mommy. Please listen to me. Never in a million years did I mean the stuff I said. I love you, mommy. More than anything. I could never hate you." For the first time, she seemed to actually hear my words. With tears welling up in her eyes, she could do nothing but nod. That's when Princeton decided to intervene and change the subject to something way lighter.

"I asked you guys to be here because me and Peyton... well we're about to embark on a new journey. I know how important family is to her, and I really believe that you all should be included in this new part of our lives. Grabbing my hand and bringing it to his face, it seemed to be then that my parents figured out what was going on. Mostly because my mom saw the rock resting on my finger.

"You're getting married?!" fanning her eyes, I laughed when she became emotional only because she reminded me so much of myself. She was a god-fearing woman, who also happened to be a hopeless romantic. "Don't you think you're a little young, Pey? You don't want to live your life a little bit more?" she asked. I knew she was just being concerned like a mother should. Like I would for Taylen, but I wasn't trying to hear all of that. I shook my head and began to talk, just as the waitress came back with our food and sat it down right in front of us.

"My life is with Princeton, mom. Actually no, fuck that. A life without Princeton is a life I'm not willing to live. He is the only man who has ever loved my daughter. He is there every morning with her, every night. He comforts her when she cries and to this day, he has been the only person that I could ever count on when it came to doing something for her. So no, I'm not too young. I want to spend my life with Princeton as my husband." I hadn't meant to curse and my words may have come out harsh, but it seemed that I got the point across because my mom nodded in approval and didn't say anything else. Next, it was my father's turn to speak and surprisingly, he wasn't as negative as I thought he would be. Leaning over and looking Princeton dead in the eyes, he nodded his head as well.

"Young man, I told my wife after you had called us that there was something about you that I liked. Something that was special about you. With that being said, let me let you know, son... There is nobody in the world more important to me than my girls. Even with everything going on and the troubles we've faced, I wish nothing but happiness and prosperity for Peyton. If you hurt her..." That's when Princeton laughed, and I could tell my parents were caught off-guard.

"Mr. Ever, trust me. You don't have to worry about that. That's not me. Besides... when I told you that we were embarking on a new journey, I meant that seriously." He smiled and looking at me, I knew exactly what he was about to say. Even though we had decided not to announce it, there was no better time than the present. Grinning at eachother, he grabbed my hand and locking our fingers together, placed it on my stomach.

"We're pregnant."

Chapter Twenty-Three:
"Is This Wandering Romance?"
Princeton James Parrish.
54 Days Later.

I felt Peyton before I saw her and I watched everyone's eyes light up as I turned around and watched her come down the aisle. She was more beautiful than I could have ever imagined. She'd chosen to go with no make-up just as I asked her and she looked even better for it.

The lighting naturally lit her up and I watched in anticipation as she made her way to me. I couldn't even decide what my favorite part of Peyton was. Her long, lively curls that got in my mouth when I held her at night. I loved holding them away from her neck as I kissed down her spine while I was hitting it from the back. The freckles that adorned Peyton's face and chest. She usually tried to cover them up with pointless make-up but she had no clue that I counted them while she was sleeping. If I traced over them lightly with my finger, they mimicked little constellations. If only she knew how much her and

Taylen really lit my life up.

Speaking of Taylen, the moment that she saw her mom come down the aisle, she tried to run but I snatched her up in my arms. She began to have a temper tantrum but my sister grabbed her and Taylen immediately calmed down. When Peyton and her father got halfway down the aisle, I started to walk towards them just like we'd practiced during the rehearsal. I shook Justin's hand firmly, silently agreeing to love and respect his daughter. When he went back to his wife's side after turning their daughter over to me, I watched tears stream down their faces. I could only imagine how they felt, considering how much time they'd wasted treating Peyton like shit. But it was a good thing all of that was over now. Grabbing her hand, I kissed it softly as I helped her walk up to stand in front of the pastor with me. I should've known her emotional ass would be crying so when I saw that tears were already starting to slide down her beautiful face, I leaned into her and made sure to wipe them away.

"You look stunning." I whispered in her ear. Knowing that I would have everyone gasping and gossiping, I refrained from kissing her even though I just wanted to pull Peyton into my arms and kiss her until she was breathless. But since that was off limits, I did the second best thing. I leaned down and planted a large, long kiss on Peyton's stomach, making sure to greet my second favorite girl in the entire world, Tajah Peace Parrish. Just like her name suggested our second daughter was the olive branch we needed to extend between us and a lot of people. Peyton's parents were ecstatic about the wedding and the new baby, surprisingly. But the most important thing to me was that they were willing to move on and work on their relationship with Peyton, my wife. *Damn, that shit sounded good as hell.*

Shondell had taken my advice and went back home, not wanting any further issues with me. She didn't know it, but I'd saved all of our communications and if she ever came within fifty yards of my family or I again, she'd be arrested in seconds. After everything that had transpired, you better believe I had security everywhere in order to protect mine. Even if you didn't see them, I could assure you they were there.

Standing back up to look my soon-to-be wife in her eyes, I couldn't help but smile. Everything the pastor was saying went through one ear and out of the other . I didn't care for all that romantic stuff but because I knew it made Peyton happy, I agreed to go all out.

"Do you promise to love and cherish your wife,

Peyton Tahj Ever for as long as you both shall live?" I finally tuned back in just in time to pull Peyton's body closer to me.

"I do..." I knew that there was a specific time for me to kiss her and as stupid as it sounded to me, I was counting down the moments in my head, eagerly waiting for the pastor to stop running his mouth so that I could kiss the air out of Peyton.

"And how about you, Peyton? Do you take your husband, Princeton James Parrish-," I laughed when Peyton immediately began to wave him off, interrupting the flow of the entire ceremony.

"I do, I do. I promise you I would not be up here if I didn't. Now can we please hurry up so I can eat? I'm growing a whole human inside of me." She snapped. The audience began cracking up and even the pastor chuckled. He'd already expected her to be a handful, since she'd had a whole lot to complain about during the rehearsal dinner the night before. That quickly changed when we got back to the hotel and I got her to fix her attitude.

"I now pronounce you husband and wife. You may kiss your bride, Princeton." I know nobody was expecting it because Peyton looked like her stomach would explode any day now, but I kissed her until her knees wobbled and then I lifted her up quickly, like she weighed less than a feather and then headed out of the church. We had a reception to attend before we headed off to our babymoon, and we'd get there, but I needed one moment alone with my now-wife before the rest of the madness started. The entire day had been full of unnecessary drama and chaos, that I specifically hired someone else to deal with so Peyton wouldn't be so stressed and cause any harm to our unborn baby girl. Today had been so wreckless that I was sure we forgot the reason that both of us were there. To be united and joined, legally and in God's eyes, as one union. For Peyton to be Mrs. Parrish though in my opinion, she'd been that since I met her. Finally placing her feet on the ground when we got to the car, I ushered her in as we snuck away from everyone else, though it was no secret. My driver already had the directions to where I wanted to go, so the moment that the door shut, he took off. I could tell Peyton's feet were hurting, since she decided to wear heels though I reminded her to be as comfortable as possible, so I threw her heels onto the floor of the limo and began rubbing them down, feeling stress melt away from her body with each stroke of my hand. Small, gentle moans escaped her mouth and only had me ready for us to get to our destination. When I felt the limo stop, I passed two crisp hundred-dollar bills to the driver through the partition and he got out, wandering around as we stayed in the car. I could tell Peyton wanted to say something but the pleasure from her feet being rubbed down distracted her momentarily. Since I told the driver to give us an hour in the back, I knew we had time.

I could feel Peyton's feet throbbing in my hands but I craved feeling something else, so while I rubbed her foot with one hand and reached under her dress, pulling her panties down to her ankles. For a moment, I thought she'd resist but it would have been pointless. She knew what she was doing with all that moaning and the sexual tension was thick enough to cut it with a knife. Laying back, Peyton rubbed her stomach and closed her eyes as I spread her legs apart and went to work. I knew that the seat would be soaked but hell, that's what I paid a deposit for so I knew they would clean it up. The more I played with her clit with my finger, the wetter she got. That's when I decided to let her see where we were.

"Mama, roll the window down." I ordered her, though Peyton was too busy trying to suffocate herself with her dress in her mouth. "Put that shit down Pey, and roll the window down. Look where we're at." The moment that she did, I held down her legs so that she couldn't free herself and tears rolled down her face.

"Why are we here?" she cried, doing her best to hold it together. I knew that this place held a special moment in our history and the fact that this was our wedding day only made it more special. I looked out the window at the sign. *1465 Chester Avenue. Cleveland Bus Station.*

"This is where it all started, Peyton. This is where our story started." I spoke as I kissed on her thighs. Right when I went back to eating her out, she began to kick and flail, her hand trying to press my head away to ease her torment. That's when I pinned her down. "No, Peyton. You've ran from me long enough. No more running. Promise me you won't run any more, from me. From us."

"Mmm... oh, God! I promise. I promise, Princeton. I won't run any more."

The End.

Chapter Twenty-Four

"TAKE ON MY LOVE."

PEYTON TAHJ PARRISH.

11 months later…

How much good not running did me. Now, look at me. Damn near twenty years old and about to deliver my third child. "You got this, Peyton. Just breathe. Just breathe. You know what to do." Princeton coached me as I focused on breathing in through my nose and out of my mouth. Though I'd done this twice before, this third time was the charm. Princeton's namesake, our son, was the reason that we were only having three children. Especially since I'd had three kids in under two years. Despite the pain of the intense contractions, I just focused on getting my sin into the world safely. Nothing could ruin this moment. Hearing the door open, I rocked back and forth as PJ tried to comfort me. The nurse on duty walked up to my bed but before she could fully pull the covers off of me, I snatched it back.

"Don't touch me." I growled, hoping she sensed the warning and backed out of my space. She did, momentarily, until my husband intervened and came to the aid.

"Peyton, let the nurse do her job, mama." He scolded me like a child. Had I not been curled up like a baby trying to handle the pain that was now coming to me in waves, I would have tried to find something sharp to stab him with. But just as I got that thought, another contraction hit me and reminded me that I had bigger worries. I just wanted to get our first-born son here safely. I wanted to hold him in my arms and kiss on his face. Just by the ultrasounds, I could tell he had my chubby cheeks. Hearing a knock on the door, I tried to turn but was still too paralyzed by the pain. My knees buckled and I cried out to God. With Taylen, I was in labor for nearly 14 hours. With Baby Taylah, who was only ten months old, it turned out to be only six. But Princeton, it seemed like his was going to be a different story. Nearly 39 hours and the end was finally in sight.

"Hi, Mrs. Ever…" I heard Princeton greet and my body instantly relaxed. Hearing my mom's name made my mood instantly change. I turned my body just enough to see my dad walk in slowly behind her. I could tell that he was uncomfortable but him just being in the room meant the world to me.

"Peyton Tahj, are you in here giving the nurses a hard time?" Princeton chuckled, and the nurse emitted a sigh, but me cutting my eyes at her lead to her shutting up halfway. I dared her to say something so I could cuss her out. Luckily for her, she remained quiet as she left the room.

"Mommy, I'm so glad you're here." I groaned, getting on my hands and knees as that seemed to be the most comfortable position. I readjusted myself again and my mom frowned as she helped me reposition my body. When she went to adjust my blanket back over my legs and my butt, her eyes nearly dropped out of her head. She turned to my dad and Princeton peeked to see what was going on. I couldn't see anything so I was relying on someone to tell me what was happening.

"Baby, go get the doctor." She directed my dad to who nearly ran out of the room.

"Mom, PJ, somebody tell me what's going on. What is it? What's wrong?" I cried. The burning sensation was getting stronger but when I looked at my mom, her facial expression didn't invoke me to panic at all. Instead, she guided my hand down between my legs so I could feel what they saw. I instantly burst into tears feeling all of the hair on my baby's head. I could hear my dad calling for help down the hallway but I knew just like my mom knew there was no time. My baby was on his way. Instead of waiting, I pushed relentlessly and after five minutes, Princeton caught our son in his hands. Just as the nurses and ny dad ran back into the room. Snatching Princeton Tahj Parrish from my husband's arms, the nurses did their normal protocol and all three of us waited in anxiety until we heard the golden cry. The tears only got stronger when they placed him on my chest and I looked into those big brown eyes. Princeton had been emotional after our daughter's birth too, but I could tell that this was different.

"He definitely has your cheeks." Princeton smiled, kissing both of us as he beamed with pride. Taking a moment, he kissed my lips passionately as both of our mouths fought for dominance. When I finally pulled away, dizzy and on a high from the love that my husband gave me, I noticed the smirk he wore on his face.

"You better cut it out, Mr. Parrish. That's how Baby Princeton got here."

Dreams of Loving A Menace From Richmond Sneak Peek...

Much of that day is still a fuzzy blur to me. I remember being in labor for awhile. A long while. The sun set twice while we waited for the baby to finally make its appearance. It seemed like no matter how hard I pushed, the baby would not make her way out so that I could kiss those beautiful cheeks I had dreamt about. Manu swore it was a boy but since he had to keep me away from the hospitals so they wouldn't figure out what was going on, we only had old Ghanaian wives' tales to go off. I knew it was a girl though.

I'd dreamt of her every night since finding out I was pregnant and despite the circumstances and how much I hated Manu for ripping me from my homeland, I had always wanted to be someone's mother. Now, I would be. Grabbing onto the sheet, I twisted my body as I felt another pain approach me. I knew she was on her way but I was exhausted. My stomach growled, famished from only eating white rice the last couple of days. But all I could focus on was getting the pain to stop. Manu was in the corner, talking to the midwife and even though the sight of him was repulsive, I really needed someone by my side. Especially, since I was delivering his child. I could hear the drums in the background and even though they were supposed to soothe me and remind me of back home, all the beating seemed to do was accelerate the cramping in my stomach. I could hear them talking, but I needed attention more.

"Oba! I feel pressure." I screamed through gritted teeth. That seemed to get her attention and she walked quickly to me. Sticking her hand in between my legs, I tried to focus on something else, but the moment her hand entered me, I pushed back. That angered Manu and he restrained me by the wrist. Even the fact that I was carrying his baby didn't stop him from treating me as a prisoner. Oba, the respective name I gave my midwife, looked to Manu and nodded at him, signaling that it was finally time for our baby to make her arrival. I had never had any antenatal care, so I didn't know what I was having but after finding out about my expectancy, my mother called once a week to give me advice on a bunch of old Ghanaian traditions. Some of them were just basic superstitions, like making sure that I didn't look at any ugly animals or my baby would come out looking like that

particular animal. Others, I could tell Manu believed. In Ghana for example, a longer labor meant that you were unfaithful to your husband. You can only imagine the thoughts going through my mind, knowing that the moment my baby was whisked away, Manu was probably going to slap me into the next century. After all, I was in labor for almost two straight days.

Feeling the most pressure I'd felt, I pushed and pushed some more until it felt like the baby had finally come out. It turned out, that was only her shoulders so I pushed a few more times and there she was. Beautiful and so serene, just like I'd pictured her. With bright eyes that piqued with curiosity and wonder, she was the most beautiful thing I had ever laid my eyes on. Kissing her face and cheeks, Oba set our baby on top of me while she cleansed the room and then used the drums to celebrate our daughter's arrival. During Abina's blessing, I carefully counted her fingers and toes, knowing that I had to make a way. Not for me anymore but for my baby. When she was finished, she immediately picked my daughter up and then transferred her over to Manu. He handed her to two other people who whisked her out of the room as I attempted to sit up. "My baby! Where are you going with my baby? Bring Abina back, Manu!" I demanded, even though I was too weak from the long process to actually do anything about it. I managed to push myself off of the bed, but my legs went out from under me and I landed with a crash on the floor. At that moment, I felt like my uterus was about to escape out of my rear end and I sobbed in pain. Pain because I was on a cold tile floor with blood pooling under me. Pain because I had given birth to my first child without my parents there for the ceremony... Pain because I was entrapped somewhere I didn't want to be, with someone I didn't want to be with. I didn't know that would be the last time I ever saw my baby. Waking up, but still in my dream, I painfully re-lived the worst memory in my subconscience. When I came to, after having my baby ripped from my arms, Manu was sitting next to me. His head was cradled in his hand and he was silent, but his body shaking indicated that he was weeping relentlessly. I already knew that had something to do with Abina. "No!!!! NO!!!" I screamed at the top of my lungs, my voice echoing through the five-bedroom home I lived in, with my owner, his wife and their son. That's when I felt someone shaking me and I opened my eyes to see Manu, the devil himself, looking at me.

"Another bad dream, Atiya?" That's when I realized the gruesome truth. I was actually awake and still living in this harsh reality. My daughter was really gone and I was stuck, all alone.

People ask me every day, "do you miss Ghana? What was it like?" and even thought the questions come constantly, the answer never gets any easier. But it's always the same. I miss Ghana every single moment of every day. My mom, my brothers, Kobe and Kojo and my sister, Serwa, my friends.... But most importantly, I missed my freedom. I missed being able to take a walk whenever I wanted to.

I couldn't even remember the last time that I'd been out without Manu, or his wife's disapproving glare following me everywhere. I had long ago given up the thought of Adjua, Manu's wife, helping me get home. That idea had been taken, along with my soul, when I witnessed her eye me enviously as Manu had his way with me. As if I wanted it. I was quickly thrown out of my thoughts and my homesickness when I heard Adjua screaming my name.

"Atiya! Come here! The child is hungry!" Passing her young daughter off to me, Adjua huffed and left the room in a frenzy after observing me closely. When I was sure that she had left, I got comfortable in the rocking chair since I was already aware that whenever I was feeding their baby, was the only time Manu and Adjua left me in peace. Stroking Baby Adjo's hair, I removed the top half of my dress as I brought her to my breast, whispering a prayer when she began to suckle. I was no believer of taking things out on innocent babies but every time I looked at Adjo, I couldn't help but think of my own baby. The one I never got to love. I know I may have confused some of you... so let me explain.

For nearly seven years, I was considered a "trokosi". As an act of revenge against my father for taking another man's woman to bed, I was taken by Manu, one of the priests to pay for his heinous crime. My parents said that my service would protect my family from the gods' anger. But what about my anger? What about the things that happened to me? Had I no right to be angry because this was just "tradition"? Thinking about my father, bitter tears began to sting the back of my eyelids but I tried to keep myself calm. If Adjo cried, Adjua and Manu would come running and I would be punished. But as I rocked her to sleep and stared out of the window, all of the memories from that fateful day almost seven years ago came flooding back.

Volta, Ghana

May 23rd 2009 was a very special day. Not only because it was my sixteenth birthday and the day I was considered a woman, but because Papa had given me a very special gift. Finally, he decided to let me go to school and not just any regular school, but some fancy school in the United States. Ever since I was younger, my parents raved of the life that we would have if we only managed to get a new break and now I was beyond excited. This was going to be a very special move for us. As I packed my bags, I pushed the beads out of my face, knowing that I'd be in trouble if I took them off. None of my friends ever got beads in their hair for their sixteenth birthday, but mama said that was just to make me different from all the other girls. Now that I look back on it, I never saw all of the signs that were right in front of me. But how could I? They were my parents so they'd protect me, right? Wrong.

It wasn't until the time for my party arrived that I realized something was wrong. Instead of my friends from the village and my class, a group of men arrived outside my home in a large van. My mom bowed to them, which I'd never seen before and one of the older men looked at me with such vivacity that I instantly hid behind my father. Any other time, he would have shielded me from all harm. But this day was different. He immediately moved out of the way and the men rushed up to me before I could react the way my older brothers taught me and run. When he picked me up, I fought.

I scratched, I kicked, I screamed and cried while my mother watched with her hand over her mouth, as if she was actually sad. My dad was too stubborn to let a tear fall but I watched him solemnly shake his head.

"Mama! Papa! Help!!!" I cried, reaching out for my brothers who had now rushed out of our small home to see what was going on. They too were undependable because as they saw our parents' reactions, they calmed down. Still, I refused to get in the van. I held on to anything that would give me a few more minutes with my family, hoping that one of them would stop this whole thing. But they never did.

As a matter of fact, when my father realized that I was giving the men too much trouble, he silently approached me. I thought he was about to save me, like he'd done so many other times. Instead, he just delivered a large slap to the side of my face.

WHAP! A loud yelp escaped my mouth and I watched in horror as my mom fell to her knees, cradling my baby sister as she cried. Had she held on to me that exact same way, we would've never been in this situation. But, here I was. At 23 years old, I'd been nothing but a domestic servant. I'd had dreams for my life here in the United States and unfortunately, I was doing nothing but raising Manu's children. If that wasn't enough, times where he just wasn't satisfied with Adjua left me to pick up the pieces. No matter how much I screamed or cried, it didn't stop him from thrusting himself into me forcefully.

As I sat in the rocking chair to nurse someone else's child, the emotions got the best of me once again. It had been almost seven months since I fought through heaven and hell, just to not be able to see the body of my little girl for the last time. She was born healthy and well, and nobody could explain to me how she was dead by the time I woke up. Unfortunately, I couldn't question Manu or say anything bad, otherwise there would be serious hell to pay. It was no secret that Manu did what he wanted to me with no repercussions, but I guess nobody expected me to ever conceive a child from it and no matter how much that he said he hated me, I watched his eyes dance with love inside of them for the first time while he held her in his arms, and she held his finger inside her tiny hand.

I realized that Adjo was getting wet when she began to flail wildly and that's when I wiped my face to find that tears had managed to escape their way down my cheeks. I quickly wiped her off, knowing that if she cried, both of her parents would come running into the room. Feeding her until she was satisfied, I quickly handed her back to Adjua and went to my room to sew until it was time for me to prepare food for Manu and his family.

The end

Follow Myah's social media to stay updated on upcoming projects, sneak peeks, contests, and giveaways!!
IG: @my_ohmy_

FB: Myriah Westbrooks (Author Myah)

SC: @callme-pharaoh

Twitter: @MyahTheAuthor

PLEASE DON'T FORGET TO LEAVE YOUR REVIEW!

Made in the USA
Columbia, SC
25 February 2020

88367583R00117